Call Me Athena

Call Me Athena

Girl from Detroit

A Novel in Verse

Colby Cedar Smith

Andrews McMeel
PUBLISHING®

Andrews McMeel Publishing
a division of Andrews McMeel Universal
1130 Walnut Street, Kansas City, Missouri 64106

www.andrewsmcmeel.com

21 22 23 24 25 BVG 10 9 8 7 6 5 4 3 2 1

ISBN: 978-1-5248-6560-3

Library of Congress Control Number: 2020943392

Editor: Patty Rice
Art Director/Designer: Holly Swayne
Production Editor: Elizabeth A. Garcia
Production Manager: Carol Coe

This book is a work of historical fiction. Names, characters, businesses, places,
events, and incidents either are products of the author's imagination or are used
fictitiously. Certain long-standing institutions and public figures are mentioned,
but the characters in the book are a product of the author's imagination.

For my grandmother
and her six great-grandchildren.

Grief

consumes
like a brush fire.

It begins
with a glowing cinder.

You think
you can smother it
with your boot.

As you tap
and kick and stomp,
it spreads
across the grass.

Once the spark grows,
it has a will
of its own.

It changes everything
in its path.

All you can do
is stand there.

With a useless
bucket in your hands.

As you watch
the entire field
burn.

I wish

I could spin my body
so fast
it could rotate
the earth.

I wish
I could reverse
the months, the days,
the hours.

Go back
to the beginning.

I wish
it could have been
me.

Mary

DETROIT, MICHIGAN
1933

They say

twin souls
can communicate
without talking.

Marguerite and I
never stop.

Not even
when we're asleep.

I put my head
next to hers.

I imagine her thoughts
traveling faster
than the speed of light
into my brain.

All the static
vanishes
and we become a radio
tuned to the same
frequency.

I wake to a swarm

of mosquitoes
tickling my cheek
and buzzing my ears.

I swat them
from the air.

You're breathing on me.

I open one eye
and see her.

> *I'm still asleep.*

So am I.

> *Good.*

We close our eyes.

After a moment,
I feel a tickling on my cheek again.

Are you awake?

My sister is as warm
as a log on a fire.

She fuels me.

We walk down the hall

into the crowded
living room.

Shield our bodies
from our three
long-limbed
younger brothers,
who snap
and twist
against each other.

Cerberus,
the three-headed dog,
guarding the gates
of the underworld.

They look up
and greet us in unison,
Good morning!
before they rush us.

John puts me in a headlock
and tugs my braid.

Gus wrestles
Marguerite to the ground
while she kicks
herself free

until my dad
looks up
from his newspaper
and yells

STOP!

*Or I'll send you back
to the old country!*

Sometimes
I wish he would.

Our apartment

is as small
as a rabbit den.

Just like rabbits
my parents keep adding
new babies
that take up space.

I look at my mother.

Hands over her eyes,
wondering
what to do
with her brood.

Her belly swells
with yet another
mouth to feed.

Why did my parents come to America?

If I had
a quarter

for every time
I asked this question,

I'd be richer
than Henry Ford.

Mama ladles the batter

for crêpes onto the pan
and turns it—just so.

With one flick
of her wrist,
she flips
the thin
golden pancake
onto the plate.

The first one there
gets the crêpe.

So you have to be fast.

My brother Jim
wins the prize
and slathers it
with strawberry preserves.

Rolls it and eats it.

All hot
and gooey.

Not me.

I just keep grabbing
and grabbing
and placing the crêpes
in my lap.

After breakfast,
I will hide them
in my drawers
underneath
my folded clothes.

It's good to have
a crêpe on hand
when you need one.

And a few
for your sister
too.

My brother John

leans back.

His hands crossed
behind his neck.

His dirty boots
on the table.

Ρεμάλι! (Remáli!)
Slob!

My father cuffs him
on the back of the head
so hard
his teeth rattle.

Gold tokens
in a slot machine.

John sits up
and smirks
as if someone
has made a joke.

I half expect him
to spit gold coins
into his cupped hands
and scream, *Jackpot!*

Just to spite
the old man.

Mary!

I look at him sideways.

Yes, Baba?

I can't remember
the last time
he addressed me.

Dimitris Nicolaides came to the shop.
He asked about you.

My mother's eyebrows rise
as her lips form
into an "O."

I can hear the silent,

O, Mary!
O, what luck!

She clasps her
hands together.

Her mind slowly opening
a cedar dowry chest
as she prepares
to make
my wedding bed.

A husband.

An old, rich, *Greek*
husband.

To put me
in my place.

Your eyes are the color of cultures clashing

she says,
as she kisses me between my lashes.

The dark brown
of the Greeks
mixed with the stormy gray
of northwestern France.

My eyes turn green
with anger.

Oh, Mary,
calm yourself.

You must
get used to the idea
of marriage.

Marguerite pats my hand.

Her eyes calm
as a fox.

Liquid pools
of the sweetest
amber.

My eyes glow
like a serpent.

The sixteen-year-old girls

in our town
are precious candies
waiting
in a crystal dish.

The boys
get to reach in,
choose
whichever treat
they want.

Marguerite
will be taken
by a man
from a good family.

She is sweet
and brings a smile
to your mouth.

When I talk,
boys look like
they've bitten
on something
bitter.

I imagine I'm pulling on a silk dress

with a feathered boa
and matching slippers.

Instead,
I squeeze into a wool dress
that is two sizes
too small.

The fabric
barely buttons across
my growing breasts.

I am filled with defeat
even before I arrive
at the battlefront.

School.

I tuck
mother's rouge,
a secret,
into my pocket.

Secure my stockings
with hidden red ribbons
around my thighs.

A little color
just for me.

I try to fix my hair

never sleek
and kept.

A dark-brown,
wild, tickling
monster
that longs
for the inside
of my mouth.

I've always felt
a woman's power
is in her hair.

The problem is

I have more of it
than most.

And I have no idea
how to tame it.

We climb down the stairs

pass through
our father's store
and enter
the busy street.

Our neighborhood
smells like
trash
metal and oil
ammonia
slaughtered chickens
and roasted goat meat.

Folks
from Greece,
Romania, Poland, and Mexico,
and many Black families
who've come up from the South
inhabit
the row houses and duplexes
along our street.

Most of our neighbors
came to Detroit
because Ford
paid his workers well.

$5 a day.

Word spread far and wide.

My mother says
I'll never have to travel
to learn
the ways of the world.

The whole world lives in Detroit.

For twenty years

the factories fed
and nourished
every part of this town.

Food on the table.
Money in the schools.
Doctors for the sick.

Every morning
the citizens
walked in one direction
toward the factory floors.

The River Rouge.

Animals gathering
at the watering hole.

Detroit drank deep.

Sustenance.

Now,
water is scarce.

We pray the source
won't run dry.

Marguerite and I hold hands

as we pass the lines.

Neighbors wait
in the courtyard
of the
Sacred Heart Church.

A nun
ladles soup
into wooden bowls.

The priest rips bread
and places it
into waiting mouths.

A woman stands
on a soapbox,
speaking so vehemently
spittle flicks
from her teeth.

I say to you, it is easier
for a camel
to go through the eye of a needle,
than a rich man to enter
into the kingdom of God! [1]

It's difficult to decide

where to look.

A town
of weathered tents
lines the streets.

Families living
in the dirt.

Women beg
for coins
with their children
on their laps.

Children
so thin
you can see their bones
through their
worn shirts

skin peeling
from sitting in the sun

teeth brown
from hunger.

A hollow-cheeked man sits
underneath a cloth banner
that reads,

Hoover's poor farm.

He holds a cardboard sign
painted with angry words
about our last president.

Hard times are still Hoovering over us. [2]

His son
stands beside him.

He bounces a ball
and chants,

Little Pig, Little Pig, let me in!
Not by the hair of my chinny chin chin!
Then I'll huff and I'll puff
and I'll blow your house in! [3]

Folks know

once you
find yourself
sitting on the road
in Hooverville, [4]

it's hard
to get back
on your
feet.

I hear a rumble behind us

I look up
to see a boy
my age.

Driving
a brand-new, red
Ford Cabriolet.

Through the open cab
I can see
his pinstriped suit.

He looks
as if he has never had
to worry.

Curly blond hair
bounces
as he speeds
down the road.

The rest of us
getting covered
in dust.

When we get to school

two boys
are dragging each other
through the yard.

Gus climbs on top
and pulls them apart.

He winds up with a bloody lip
before the bell rings.

We file into
the classroom.

I hear Evie Williams
talking about me.

Two sizes too small!
You can see EVERYTHING!

Her friend Fay
looks at me
and mouths
an apology.

Evie stares
at the popping buttons
on my dress.

Eyes wide
like the barrel
of a gun,
loaded
and ready
to fire.

My whole body
feels hot
and panic
swells my brain.

I am a sack of grain
with a target
painted
on my chest.

I settle on a bench

between Marguerite
and Elena.

Elena's parents
are from Romania.

She was born
in America
just like us.

Elena's cheeks
are ripe, round
plums.

Her black, straight hair
smells like cooked
cabbage.

We link
our elbows together.

If our school
were a garden,
I think Elena,
Marguerite, and I
would be growing
on the very same
vine.

We rise and pledge

allegiance
to the flag
of the United States
of America.

We all speak
in different accents.

Our voices ring
in unison.

Liberty and justice
for all.

For a brief moment,
it feels like
we might
have something
in common.

Then I see Evie
sneering at me again.

CAREER

Our teacher, Mrs. Patterson,
scribbles the word
on the blackboard.

Asks us to write
a paragraph about what
we want to do
when we graduate.

What are your dreams?

My brothers
start writing immediately.

John wants to be a pilot.
Gus wants to be a soldier.
Jim wants to build skyscrapers.
Marguerite wants to be
a homemaker.

I don't write anything.

Good Greek Girls
know better than to dream.

Good Greek Girls

never speak before spoken to.

Good Greek Girls
never ride bikes.

Good Greek Girls
marry at a young age.

Good Greek Girls
take care of the babies at home.

Good Greek Girls
don't have jobs.

Good Greek Girls
don't dance and smoke and drink.

Good Greek Girls
never complain.

I don't know if I want to be
a Good Greek Girl.

My mother calls her daughters

to the kitchen.

We carry serving dishes
filled with
stuffed tomatoes and peppers
and large bowls
of cucumber salad.

We eat outside
in my father's garden
under the climbing grapevines.

Amidst the aroma
of the blooming roses
and carnations
planted
to remind him
of Greece.

My mother loves
when we eat and drink
and laugh together
at the table.

After dinner,
she serves
the bright-red cherries
that we canned
last fall.

She ladles them
into small crystal bowls
with silver spoons

souvenirs

memories
from her life
in France.

I saw a fight in town

my brother Gus says
from the corner of a full mouth
as he reaches
for a second helping
of cherries.

My mother glares at him.

A real doozy.
The whole works.

One guy was calling
the other guy names.

He didn't like it much.
Pulled out a blade.

The crowd gathered in a circle
around them.

I didn't stay
to see how it turned out.

He shovels more fruit
into his mouth

and doesn't notice
the bloodred juice
staining his chin.

My father holds his worry beads

clicks them
between his forefinger
and his thumb.

Too many men
out of work.

His voice
accents each word
like the beads
on the string.

The factories
were the only thing
keeping peace
in this town.

My mother puffs air
out of her mouth
in exasperation,

Now everyone is praying
that the immigrants
will go home.

This is our home.

What would it feel like

to have blond hair and blue eyes?

My sister asks
with a dreamy voice.

I look at Marguerite's
big, beautiful, black, curly hair.

Her amber eyes
and olive skin.

I can't help laughing.

What would it feel like
to have a name
like Smith or Jones?
I retort.

What would it feel like
to have great-great-grandparents
who arrived on the Mayflower?
she giggles.

What would it feel like
to drink Coca-Cola
at the beach
under an umbrella?

I act like I'm opening
a parasol.

What would it feel like
to not speak Greek,
eat Greek food,
go to Greek church?

Normal?
my sister asks.

"Normal" is not a word
I have ever used.
I say with a flourish.

I take her hand
and spin her
around the yard.

There's a pharmacy and a soda shop

on the corner.

Marguerite and I
don't have the ten cents
to buy a copy of

Ladies' Home Journal

so we stand in the aisle
and suck
penny candies
and read the articles,

"Keep That Wedding Day Complexion"[5]
"A Man's Idea of a Good Wife"
"Hints and Suggestions for Helpful Girls"

Just as we are about
to dig into
a particularly juicy story,

"Promiscuous Bathing"[6]

Mrs. Banta,
the owner's wife,
finds us huddled
in the corner whispering.

She sweeps us out
of the doorway
with her broom.

We look into the shop windows

to examine ourselves.

Dab our lips and cheeks
with red rouge.

We pose like starlets
in the magazine.

Jazzy flappers.

Imagine
we have short, cropped curls
and flasks
tucked into
our knee-highs.

Girls who drive
in cars with boys
and dance.

Come look!

I pull Marguerite's arm
until we're standing
in front
of a dress shop.

A mannequin
with a surprised expression
gestures
toward the heavens
like she just felt
the first
drop of rain.

An emerald green
evening dress
draped
across her form.

Rose beige
patent leather
T-straps.

A gardenia
in her hair.

Oh, Marguerite!
Isn't she divine?

    She's beautiful.

I wish
we had matching dresses
just like this
and a place to wear them.

    I wish we had new boots.

I look down
at our worn boots
and my dreams
fizzle.

The clouds turn gray
and disappointment
falls
from the sky.

Our boots are practical

Black.
Sturdy.
Thick soles.

They're meant to last.

We will wear them
until the thread unspools
and the leather cracks.

Until the rainwater
soaks through
and our bones
are cold.

We will stuff them
with newspaper.

It won't make a difference.

Only then
will we beg our mother
for a new pair.

She will look
at all of our shoes
and decide.

Whose feet are the coldest.
Whose lips are the bluest.

Who needs the warmth
the most.

After church on Sunday

there is a man waiting
at the carved doors
of the entryway.

My father embraces him.

Dimitris takes my hand
and brushes it
with his dry lips.

His striped vest
bulges
with his belly fat.

Dimitris tells me
he owns a shop,
a haberdashery.

He sells men's clothing.

Silk and felt hats
of all shapes and sizes.

Fabric and thread
ribbons and zips
buttons and clasps
and small notions.

Dimitris lives alone.

In a sad house
that smells like
soup.

I tell my father

if that man
comes in the front door,
I will go out
the back.

My mother yanks me

into the kitchen.

Control your temper.

My sister
is peeling carrots
at the table.

In my frustration
I blurt out,

What about Marguerite!

*Why doesn't she
have to get married?*

As soon
as the words
come out of my mouth,
I feel sorry.

Marguerite
looks up from
her work
with a panicked
expression.

A fox
caught in a snare.

*I am more concerned
about you, Mary!*
my mother snaps.

*What man
would choose a girl
like you?*

I imagine the day of my wedding

I walk down the aisle
toward a man
I do not love.

Surrounded
by hallowed images.

The priest blesses us
as the chorister chants,

*Ησαϊα χόρευε,
η Παρθένος έσχεν εν γαστρί.*
*(Isaïa chóreve,
i Parthénos éschen en gastrí.)*
*Isaiah dance,
the Virgin is with child.*

He signs the cross
and lays a wreath
of flower buds
on my black curls.

Another
on the gray hair
of my groom.

Entwined together
by the Father, the Son,
and the Holy Spirit.

We drink from one cup.

Servants of God.

Marguerite is lying on her back

in the garden.

Her arms and legs
spread like a starfish
on a rock.

I lay down beside her.

We look like stars
in the same constellation.

I don't want to leave.
I don't want to get married.

I'm happy in this home
with you.

She holds my hand
and says,

It can't stay the same forever.

Even if
we wish it could.

I feel like someone
has thrown a stone
into the heavens
and smashed the stars.

We are falling
from the sky.

I lie for a long time in the grass

even after Marguerite has gone.

I turn on my shoulder
and spy a shovel
lying on the ground.

I stand and pick it up.

Walk down the cellar steps
to return it to where
it belongs.

The cellar smells
of the dark, moss, fungus
that lives
in the packed dirt floors
of this subterranean space.

Shelves hold
boxes of potatoes,
garlic, apples, and onions.

I lean
the heavy shovel
against the wall
and it falls
with a loud crash
onto a shelf.

Boxes topple down.

Heads of garlic
fly across the floor.

I groan and bend to gather
the rolling bulbs
when I notice
an ancient wooden box
covered in dust.

The clasp sprung open.

A stack of letters
tumbling
onto the ground.

I hold an envelope in my hand

There's no name
no address
no stamp.

I open
the folded paper
and begin to read.

Letter #1

My dearest,

I woke this morning afraid. No one knows where you are.

How can I find you?

I don't even know where to send this.

I pray you are alive.

Always Yours,
Petit Oiseau

Letter #2

October 10, 1918

Love of my life,

Lying in this field surround by smoke and fire, I feel as if our moments together never existed.

How could I have been so happy? Loved you so innocently?

I am sure by now the bed that I slept in is occupied by another wounded man.

Have you forgotten me?

I am afraid I will become what I most fear.

Le Loup

I read

until my eyes blur.

My skin grows cold
with cellar
darkness.

Who were these people?

Where are they now?

Giorgos (Gio)

KOMNINA, CENTRAL GREECE
1915

The church bells chime

through the windows
of our house on the hill.

My mother
hums softly,
a song she repeats night
after night
until it becomes a part of me
and the air we breathe.

It feels as if the wind
might come from the sea
and take me on its back

a white Pegasus
or a boat,
with wings
for sails.

I go to school with the mountains

the rocks
the olive trees
that grow in a tangled grove
next to our house.

My teachers are the lizards
that love the dusty soil
and explore the world
with their flicked
tongues.

I go to school
without books
without the brick walls
of a building
with my fifteen-year-old twin,
Violetta.

Wiry and tough.

Her hair braided
in a black crown.

A sweet-smelling halo
curled around
her head.

Mother asks us

to gather quail eggs
from the low grasses and scrub
on the hillside.

We listen
for the *chuck-chuck-chuck*
of the hen
as she scratches out
hidden hollows
at the bottom
of a tree trunk.

Startled,
she leaps into the air
in a quick burst
of flight.

We see
the brown and white
speckled eggs
camouflaged
against
the undergrowth.

Still warm from
their mother's breast,
we cradle them
in our palms.

As we walk away,
guilt rips
at my chest.

The thought
of the mother
frantically searching
for what
has been lost.

Giorgos, come quick!

Violetta has found a cave.

There are wild animals,
beasts,
that live in these hills.
Muscled cats, brown bears,
and jackals.

We imagine
the great Spartan warriors
of Thermopylae.

We enter the mouth of the cave.

All we find
is a γίδα (gída),
a small goat.

Her bell jingles
from a leather strap
wrapped
around her neck.

She is staked to the ground.

Miles of wilderness.
No freedom.

A circle of grass
mowed down
around her.

We name the goat Alethea

It means truth.

She is stubborn.
She will eat your clothes.

And also trash.

You have to watch her closely.

She's always trying
to get away
with something.

I scratch her
and she curls her head closer
to my hand.

When I stop
she stares at me
with her vertical
amber eyes.

A creature
from the underworld
who knows
everything

but will tell me
nothing.

The old men in the village

are sighing
and talking about war.

The elders know what is coming.

Young men puff up their chests.
They will join the army.

I do not want to fight.

Why do I need to carry a gun
to prove
that I love my country
and my home?

Violetta ties her skirt

in a knot between her legs.

She wants to wear
pants instead
of the dress and apron
she must wear
everyday.

She puts on my vest and hat
when our mother is out.

Ὦπα! (Hopa!), she says.
I look very brave!

One day, Violetta falls asleep
wearing my clothes.

My mother comes
home.

She spits
in Violetta's face,
*Our house will be shamed
because of you!*

I wipe the tears
from Violetta's eyes.

She would be
a very brave boy indeed.

When my mother's eyes are red

like the juice of a blood orange,

that is how I know
she has been crying.

She tries to do it in secret,
but we all know it happens.

She misses my father.

She never says
that she loved him,
only that he was good
to her.

Most of the men from the village
are not good to their wives.

One time, I saw a man
throwing stones at his wife
while she covered her head
with her hands.

One day, I will become a man.
I will try to be good.

There are stories

of dolphins
and mermaids

who push
their heads
out of the water.

Offer
their breath
to men
who are
drifting.

Sometimes
I wonder
if this happened
to my father.

Perhaps
they saved him
and took him

to an island
with fresh water
and fruit growing
on trees.

I like to think of this.

Rather than his boat
on the bottom
of the sea.

My sister and my mother

clean the house
bake the bread
feed the animals
milk the goat
tend to the garden.

I am not allowed to help.

If I lift a plate,
my mother slaps my hand
and screeches,
Women's work!

I hear the crack
of my mother's voice,
Violetta! Come!

I watch
the anger rise
on my sister's pink cheeks
like she has been struck
by a willow switch.

My mother has found a match

for Violetta.

She clasps her hands in triumph
and grins as widely
as a fisherman's net
spread across
a harbor.

He's from a good family!
I have been listening at the market,
I have been talking to the women.

She will go to a good home
to a man
who will care for her!

We will wait
until you turn sixteen,
my mother says.

Her hands
placed firmly on her hips.

My sister puts her cheek
on the cool
wooden table.

Mother spoons
large portions
of tomatoes, feta,
and beans
onto our plates.

She does not see
that my sister
has completely
lost
her appetite.

I find my sister

in the garden.

She's holding a small bouquet
of wildflowers.

*I don't know why
I picked these.*

They will wilt by tomorrow.

I put my hand
on her shoulder.

Think of all the words
that could comfort.

None of them seems right.

She holds the flowers
out to me.

*They would have been happier
staying right where
they were.*

My father told me

the three most important
things in life:

the boat, the sea,
the family.

That's all you need.

My father is missing

My sister is about to leave me.

And I don't have
a boat.

Jeanne

The smell of the sea

climbs the walls
of our city
like a salty,
dangerous
pirate

who steals
into my bedroom
and whispers
in my ear.

Come with me.

The night turns me
into a sparrow.

Wings tipped
with golden arrows.

The stars sing
in the firmament
a song that belongs
to me alone.

Come home.

We live in a house

on the top of a hill

filled with beautiful
things

and a maid
to dust them.

We live in a house

with a small black dog
named Felix
who eats
out of a crystal bowl.

We live in a house

filled with visitors
who drink champagne
and dine on oysters
and canapé
in the rose garden.

We live in a house

as old as the cathedral

with a balcony door
that opens
to the emerald sea.

We live in a house

filled with books,
tales of adventures
and voyages.

I wonder
if these stories
will ever be written
about me.

A letter arrives

Papa breaks a government
red wax seal
to open it.

He is needed in the war effort.

They know
he will be a wonderful doctor
in the French Foreign Legion.

It is time
for him to fulfill his duty
to his country.

He will leave
the day after Christmas.

He throws the letter
into the fire.

It crackles and spits
and rises up the chimney,
black as smoke.

It is mid-December

and we gather
with our neighbors
for *la fête de Noël,*
our winter festival.

It is my favorite day
of the year.

We eat crêpes filled
with sugar and jam
and *galettes saucisses,*
spiced sausages.
Drink cider and *chouchen,*
a honey brew.

My father's friends
pat him on the back,
wish him luck.

Neighbors
thank him for his service.

The music begins.

We laugh and breathe hard
as we dance and sing
in a circled chain
to the bagpipes, the accordion,
the fiddle, and the drum.

Two sisters join the stage
and sing
an a cappella song.

We stop to listen.

Their voices wind
around each other,
a threaded bobbin
whirling inside
a spinning wheel.

They sing *le chant des marins.*

A sailor's song
for our people. [7]

The Bretons

are wild
like the purple heather
that grows
on our rocky shore.

The Bretons

are sweet
like the gold
we squeeze
from the depths
of the honey's lore.

The Bretons

are brave
as the northern wind
and we know that
we must pray.

To the Lord, our God

to keep our ships
from that dark
and watery grave.

O keep us from
that watery grave.

O keep us from
that grave.

Maman closes her eyes

I see tears escape.

We listen to the music,
but I know we are both
thinking of the boat
that will take Papa
to a country
far from here.

She hugs me close.

My head fits perfectly
in the curve of her neck.

I can hear
her heart
beating.

A lonely bird
trapped in a cage.

The day before

my father leaves,
the townspeople gather

to see Louis Blériot
and his amazing
flying machine,
the *Blériot XI.*

My father and I
join the crowd
to watch
as the daring Frenchman
turns on the throttle
and steps
to the propeller.

With several huge pulls,
the airplane begins
to hum
like a swarm of hornets.

I grab my father's hand,
frightened by the sound.

He shouts into my ear,
Don't you see, chérie?
This will help us win the war.

Commandeur Blériot
places his goggles
over his eyes
and waves to the crowd
before he mounts
the open frame
of the two-seater plane.

Within moments,
he speeds straight ahead
into the fallow field
and lifts
into the bright,
blue sky.

On the way home

my father
places his arm
around my shoulders.

I have to go,
mon petit oiseau.

I nod
as tears escape.

I have been trained to heal people.

His voice breaks.

I will try my best
to make you proud.

He looks
over the walls of our city
to the ocean
beyond.

I don't want to leave you
and Maman.

I put my arms
around his neck
and he lifts me
off the ground.

Tears roll down my cheeks
onto the shoulder
of his suit.

I will try
to make you proud too,
Papa.

My mother dresses me

in my best dress.

Black stockings
and black-buttoned boots.

A large white ribbon
tied on the top
of my auburn curls.

I look like a present.

I wish
she would let me
sweep my hair up
on the top of my head.

Instead,
she dresses me
like a toddler.

We hear
the whistle
loud and clear.

My father points
through
the crowd of people
on the dock
and says,

*See that
beautiful boat, chérie?*

*It's going to take me
all the way
to Siam.*

That night I dream of water

I am a selkie.

Half-girl and half-seal
who has found
her white coat
and can finally return
to the sea.

I swim alongside
my father's boat,
jumping
in the foam waves
as the ship cuts
across the dark water.

I can save him
if he needs to be saved.

Up above,
an airplane looms,
sputtering
its hot fumes
into the clean air.

I wake
in sorrow.

I am just a girl.

Letter #3

October 12, 1918

My darling, my love,

My hands are so cold I can hardly hold a pen.

I worry you will never get this.

You will never know how much I loved you.

Will these pages end up scattered like poppies across a field?

Perhaps they belong to no one.

Only God and the wind.

Your always faithful,
Loup

Letter #4

October 15, 1918

Every day, I grow more tired.

Tired of waiting. Tired of the war. Tired of my own loneliness.

How could you have left me without a word?

I am without a husband, without a father, without faith.

Living in a city surrounded by granite walls.

Did you ever love me, at all?

Forever yours,
Petit Oiseau

I fold the letters, exactly as they were

return them
to their hiding place

a doorway into

another time,
another world.

These notes
are not meant for me.

I am intruding,
spying
far beyond
into someone else's life.

Marguerite's footsteps
on the back steps
wake me from my dream.

I emerge from the cellar
just in time.

Ready to go to school?

I want to tell her about the letters.

The envelopes
without addresses,
without stamps.

Written long ago.

My mouth stays sealed.

Mrs. Patterson tells us to be proud

We live in the City of Transportation.

Founded on
Henry Ford's
original idea.

The busy hands of builders
forge and lathe, work and tend,
spin and weave, form and transform
the ideas of men into objects
for the world. [8]

She stands
in front of the class.

Her hands clasped
under her chin.

Wonder spreads
across her face
as she says,

We are proud of our city
and our brothers and fathers

who have built
the foundation

of our modern
nation.

Yes. We are proud

of our brothers and our fathers.

But I want to ask:

What about
our sisters and our mothers?

Who carry generations
in their wombs

who rise and feed us,
clothe us,
and tend to us

who birth each day
into being?

She calls me to the front

of the class.

Mary, please list
the ways
Henry Ford
and the factories in Detroit
are helping
America's economy.

My heart flutters
as I walk
to the board.

She hands me
a piece of chalk.

It rolls
out of my hand
onto the floor.

I reach down,
balance on one foot.

Barely reach
for the chalk
and . . . rip.

Just like
a molting insect
that has grown
too large
for its shell,
my dress
tears
down my back.

Everyone in the class
laughs.

Especially Evie,
whose long arms
are spread
across her desk.

A spider poised
and ready
to eat me.

Elena stands up.

Leads me
back to the bench
with Marguerite
who wraps
her sweater around me
in a hug.

My mother claws through

her bulging basket
of fabric scraps.

Chooses a triangle
of dark-brown corduroy.

Stitches it
into the seam
of my shredded dress.

I try it on
to make sure it fits.

I am a walking quilt.

To console me

she lets me sit on the counter
while she makes
the baklava
for the store.

She gives me
the first piece.

As I bite into it,
the honey drips
down my arm.

I am as happy
as a bear
that has stolen
a honeycomb
from a hive.

In the store, we sell:

1. fruits and vegetables
2. soap for dishes
3. soap for laundry
4. coffee and tea
5. candy
6. whole watermelons
   and cold soda pop,
   submerged in a big case
   filled with water and ice
7. cans of soup
8. loaves of bread
9. pickles and eggs, in large barrels
   filled with brine
10. meat, which my father carves
    at the wooden counter
11. feta, a Greek cheese
12. spanakopita, a delicious spinach pie
13. moussaka, an eggplant casserole
14. baklava, a crispy dessert
    made with nuts and honey

I call Marguerite *Little Mama*

She loves to be in charge
of the house.

I'd rather
work at the store.

I love the smell
of the wooden floorboards

the food resting
on the counter

the sweat and perfume
of the customers.

Even the money has a smell.

Mama, do you think we could

convince father
to let me work in the store?

> Why would you
> want to work
> in the store?

I like the store.

> I need your help at home.

You have Marguerite.

> I need you both.

Mama, don't you think

it would be a good idea
for me
to learn the business?

> *Why would you want*
> *to learn something*
> *that you will never use?*

> *Learn how to feed your husband.*
> *Learn how to raise the babies.*

She pats her belly.

Then she points
her forefinger
in my direction.

> *Learn how to keep your opinions*
> *to yourself.*

Mama, I've been thinking about Dimitris

Her ears perk up.
She lifts her chin
and her eyebrows.

    Yes?

I straighten my skirt
and spine
to make myself
seem taller,
like I'm frightening
a bear.

When I marry Dimitris . . .

    Yes?

That is, if he'll have me . . .

    Yes.

*Don't you think
he would want someone
who knows something
about a store?*

The mother bear
takes two steps back.

*Lots of girls
can have babies.
Hopefully, I can.*

    Yes.

The bear stomps the ground
and snorts.

Maybe, if I can help
with Dimitris's store
it will make me seem . . .
useful?

       Yes.

Yes?

I stand behind the counter

place my palms
on the smooth varnished wood.

The store is empty
and quiet.

I take a deep breath
and savor my victory.

When I'm bored

I wipe each shelf.

Tally up receipts.

Record sales.

Dance with a mop.

Restock items.

Make tea.

Try not
to eat the candy.

Draw
monsters and angels
on the frosty
cold cases.

Look at myself
in the shiny cabinet.

Wonder
if I'm beautiful.

I also think about
what we could change
to bring more customers
into the store.

Since, it appears,
there are not
very many.

You know that look

when the sun
is horizontal in the sky

and someone is lit
from behind?

You can barely
see their face
because they are bursting
with light.

And you wish you
had a camera
to capture
all the shadows
and shine.

It was like that.

When I looked
at the shop door
there was a man
who was glowing.

I had to shield my eyes.

Light escaping
every edge
every surface.

Streaming
from his fingertips
each strand
of hair.

I couldn't
see his face
until he stopped
right in front
of me
and smiled.

Holding
a polished red apple
in his hand.

He looks American

like he was raised on a farm
in Nebraska.

Tall and blond.

I stare at his blue eyes
and white teeth.

Who are you?
I stammer.

> *I'm Billy Smith.*

What are you doing here?

> *I'm . . . buying an apple?*

He places a nickel
into my hand.

*Can I help you
find anything else?*

He flashes his smile
one more time and says,

> *I think I've found everything
> I'm looking for.*

He walks backward
five steps,
staring at me.

Turns
and walks
out of the door.

I hear an engine rumble
and make it to the window
just in time
to see the rear bumper
of his shiny, red
Ford Cabriolet.

My heart stops beating

for five seconds.

What would it feel like?

To have a name
like Smith or Jones?

I feel the weight

of the nickel.

The warmth of it.

All good shop owners know
we buy with our eyes
then our hands.

Feel the cold
pleasure
of a voluptuous grape
pinched between
our fingers.

Admire an apple
that's impossible
to indent.

Weigh
the smoothness
of a scrubbed potato.

Press
the thick skin
of a ripe melon.

Choose
what our hands
and our minds
want.

Giorgos (Gio)

The ground is covered

with pine chips
and tools.

I sand
the wood smooth.

Cut and curve
the long strips of pine.

Create a frame.

With each
movement,
I think about the day
when I will be able
to stand on the deck
of my own
wooden boat,
my *kaiki*.

Just like my father
and his father
before him.

I will feed my family
with the fish I catch
from the cerulean waters
of the
Aegean Sea.

Violetta's betrothed

invites her to take a walk.

He is twice her age.

He arrives with flowers
and a jug of wine
he has made
from the grapes
that he grows
on his land.

My mother tells me
to walk behind them
at a distance.

I clench my teeth.

Try to concentrate
on the birds
and the blue sky.

Think of stories
about how I will
stop the wedding
just in time.

I notice Violetta
smiling.
She even laughs
once.

When we return
she tells my mother
she will marry him.

Maybe
she will be happy.

Maybe
Costas will love her
and not be
the kind of man
who throws
stones.

It takes a moment

for my eyes to adjust to the dark.

The air is thick
with frankincense
and beeswax.

Every surface in the church
is painted.

Icons glimmer above
a red velvet carpet.
The dark-blue ceiling
is covered
in golden stars.

The dome of heaven.

Father Yiannis
appears
from an arched door.

His black robes
and Orthodox cross
swing back and forth
as he walks.

His furrowed brow
softens.

Giorgos! I'm so happy to see you!

He immediately puts me
to work.

I gather branches and leaves
and sweep the courtyard.

When I finish my chores
Father Yiannis
teaches me to read
and write passages
from his bible.

The old man
sits beside me.
Folds his hands
and closes his eyes
in prayer.

I break
from my work.

Father,
will my sister be happy
married to Costas?
Will she still . . .
my voice cracks,
need me?

He sighs deeply.

It is a brother's duty
to always protect
and watch over
the life of his sister.

Jesus Christ laid down his life for us.
And we ought to lay down our lives
For our brothers and our sisters.[9]

Then he stops
and sticks one finger in the air.

Life is work. Life is duty.

The important part
is to enjoy the small pleasures.

He stands up
and pours himself
a small
glass of wine
from the decanter
behind the altar.

His eyes twinkle.
Don't tell the women!

I walk down the stone steps

and almost collide
with Violetta's friend,
Mariana.

Her arms full
of folded
embroidered cloth
for the church.

Underneath
her white headscarf
I can see
there are red ribbons
woven
into her hair.

My mother and Violetta
walk behind her,
arms loaded with flowers
and Violetta's
linen wedding dress.

My mother scowls at me
and hisses,

*She has been promised
to another!*

She does not belong to you!

Violetta will have a life of her own

What will I do?

The weight of loneliness
is an anchor
pulling me
toward
the bottom
of the sea.

It feels like I cannot move.

The promise
of the current
tugs at me.

The night before the wedding

Costas arrives
with a present for Violetta.

It is a bundle
wrapped
in the soft white skin
of a lamb.

Violetta opens the package.

She runs her hands
over yards
of dark pinstriped
cloth.

Costas sits beside her.

We will wrap
the lambskin around
our first child
to keep him warm.

The fabric is for you.

You can make
a pair of pants,
and we can work
in the fields
side by side.

Violetta's eyes fill
with tears.

What will the village say?

Costas takes Violetta's hand.

I'm not marrying the village.
I'm marrying you.

The leaving ritual

Violetta kneels in the dust
in front of Alethea.

She feeds the goat a coin.

*If we give away
our most precious things,
it will bring us wealth.*

We will have everything we need and more.

She feeds the goat a flower.

*It will spread the flower's seeds into hills
beyond our home.*

We will bring beauty to the lives of others.

She feeds the goat a ring.

*A circle with no end
and no beginning.*

We will always be family.

On the day they marry

Costas wears a gray suit.

Violetta wears an embroidered red dress
with a belt made of coins.

Her head covered by the same scarf
our mother wore at her wedding.

I give Violetta to Costas.

Father Yiannis chants
and swings a golden bowl
filled with incense
blessing them both.

After the ceremony,
I cradle our goat, Alethea,
in my arms.

I thank her for her cheese
and mischief.

Soothe her
as I run the blade
along her throat.

She struggles and finally
gives her life to me.

We feed both families, our only gift.

The music begins.

One man strums a λαούτο *(laoúto)*
a long-necked lute,
while the other keeps beat
with a νταούλι *(daoúli)* drum.

We dance into the dark-blue night
in a circle
holding hands.

Jeanne

After my father leaves

my mother
takes to her bed
and cries
for two days.

We both know
life must go on.

She spends hours
in her garden
tending the sweet-smelling
roses that climb
the trellises
on the side of our house.

She clips lavender
and delphinium
and my favorite
marguerites, white daisies
with a bright-yellow
center.

She places them
in a vase
by my bedside.

She lies next to me
and curls her body
around mine.

Je t'aime, chérie.
We will survive this.

Papa is not the only one

to leave his family
behind.

There are no more men.

All of them
have gone to war.

Women drive the boats
in the harbor.

Women
butcher the meat
and run the factories.

Women
grease the rails
for the trains
at the
Gare de Saint-Malo.

Some women like the change.

They are even
wearing their husbands' suits
and ties
and smoking
thin cigars.

Not my mother.

She puts her hand
over my eyes
when they pass us
on the street.

I want to look.

I think they
are beautiful
in their pinstriped
pants.

We go for a picnic

in the country.

Lay out a blanket
in a green field.

Eat cold chicken
drumsticks
and thick slices
of Camembert cheese
smeared onto
a baguette.

My mother
takes off her shoes
and rests her head
on my lap.

For a second,
she looks like a child.

On the drive home

I see three peasant women.

They are hitched to a plow
like horses.

They pull the heavy equipment
through the fields,
carving
lines in the dark earth.

Their husbands are gone.
Their horse is gone.

But they still
need to eat.

Days pass

and leaves drift
to the ground.

The first snow falls.

Maman and I
decide to stay
on the sofa,
protected
by a warm blanket.

Instead of joining
our friends and neighbors
for *la fête de Noël.*

We both realize,
but we do not say it
aloud.

Papa has been gone
a full year.

Letter #5

October 18, 1918

Mon Petit Oiseau,

Missing you is like missing a season.

I would like to lie in the grass, eat a peach, swim in the ocean, but the gray days of winter won't leave me.

The sun never shines.

In the morning I wake, hoping for your warmth once again.

Your ever loyal,
Loup

Letter #6

I read fairy tales as a child—and I swore I would never be the damsel in distress.

The problem is this: I am alone and I miss you.

I am worried you need rescuing too.

Please come back.

I am in my tower, overlooking the ocean.

I will leave the light on so you can find me.

A meeting is arranged

My mother rakes
a comb through
my unkempt
black, curly hair.

A trainer, combing
the barn
and dust
out of a horse's
mane.

Marguerite
stands in the doorframe
looking sympathetic.

She knows
my mother's comb
is coming for her
next.

I want to lift both
my legs
and kick
like a stubborn
mule.

Not the prized
sleek
racehorse
my mother is grooming
me to be.

Why can't I choose

to marry
a man that I love?

My mother stops
brushing my hair.

She looks around
our tiny apartment,
throws her hands
in the air.

Look where that got me.

Mother slices the cake

Father pours
sour cherry liqueur
into small glasses.

Mary made this herself,
he says
and pats my arm
with pride.

Dimitris takes a sip
and smiles politely.

They leave us alone
in the parlor.

Golden icons
of Mary and baby Jesus
look down at me
from high
on the shelves.

Dimitris scoots next to me.

The side of his body
is touching mine.

You are a beautiful young girl,
he says as he takes
a lock of my hair
and twists it around
his finger.

His breath smells
like death
and onions.

Who is this wicked old man?

He wants a child.

I want
to grow the claws
and wings
of a Gorgon.

Feed his eyes
to the hungry
creatures
that live
in the depths
of the swamp.

Turn him into
stone.

When I was twelve

my mother and I
embroidered

a soft white gown,
two sheets,
and two pillowcases.

Every single piece
decorated
with pink
and yellow flowers.

We folded them
carefully
into my cedar dowry chest.

I imagined
with each stitch
how excited
I would be
to wear a nightgown
in front of a man
for the first time.

Now, I know
I have sewn
the bed
that I must
lie in.

These linens
will be my prison.

For our birthday

Mama has a surprise
for us
downtown.

As we turn the corner
we see a lighted sign:

The Showplace of Detroit
<u>Fox Theatre</u>
Most Magnificent Temple
of Amusement in the World

We enter the movie palace.

Carved golden columns
and two winged lions
guard the door.

The orchestra plays and the choir sings.

The red velvet curtain pulls aside.

The words
Le Passion de Jeanne d'Arc
scroll across the screen. [10]

Mama and Marguerite and I
hold hands and cry.

As we watch
Joan of Arc
kneel
before her accusers.

She listens
to the voices.

Listens
to the spirit she can feel
but cannot name.

Listens
to the ringing
in her ears, her heart,
her throat.

Not to the men
who are sworn to protect her.

Not to those
who would manipulate
her power.

Not to the judge
who sees her fire
burning

her strength
building

her understanding
growing.

Not to the bishop
who with a clear conscience
sends her
to the pyre.

I have always felt close to Jeanne d'Arc

my mother tells us
as we ride the streetcar home.

I wanted to be her
when I was young.

> *Why?*
> asks Marguerite.

> *She died*
> *the most horrible*
> *death!*

Yes,
but she had
the most powerful
connection
to the world
beyond.

We women have so few choices.

There was a time
when I thought I could be brave
like her . . .

She falls silent.

Then her eyes fill with light.

She holds both
of our hands
and says,

It is silly, but I believe
she watches over
all the women
in our family.

Then looks
directly at me.

Even when we must endure
that which we cannot choose.

When we arrive home

my brothers
are playing baseball
in the street.

Gus hands me the bat.

John lobs a ball.

I swing
and hit the edge,
ground it
and barely
make it
to first base.

Marguerite whoops
with excitement.

Mama! You try!
I squeal, as she heads
toward the apartment.

To my surprise,
she turns around.

Grabs the bat
and slings it
across her shoulder.

She bends her knees.
Ready.

John tosses the ball
and it connects.

It flies over all of our heads.

She smiles
as we all cheer.

She waves
to her adoring crowd
then heads up the stairs
to make dinner.

I walk toward the store

to make sure
everything is secured
for the night.

There's a piece of paper
jammed
into the door.

It has my name on it.

Marguerite and the boys
climb the stairs
to our apartment.

I call to them
as calmly
as possible,

I'll be right up.
I'm just going to check
on the shipment!

Close the door.
Sink to the floor.

I hold the letter
to my chest.

My banging
heart.

Breathe.

Open the note.

Mary,

Meet me
at American Coney Island [11]
after school
on Thursday.

I'll get us a table.

Billy

I stare at the paper

shaking in my hands.

This is not
a note from a lost time.

A note of war and sorrow.

Separation and longing.

This is a note for me.

From a real, live boy.

Who knows my name.

Giorgos (Gio)

KOMNINA, CENTRAL GREECE
1916

I help Costas

harvest olives.

We lay thick nets
beneath the branches of the trees,
then raise our rakes
and rattle them through
the sage-colored leaves.

The purple ovals
fall to
the ground.

Costas looks
across the field.

I see my sister
walking toward us.

The sun on her skin.

Her long, black hair tied
in a red scarf.

A white, billowing shirt
tucked into her new pair
of pinstriped pants.

She helps
to gather the corners
of the net
and work the fruit
to the center.

We sort the olives
from the fallen branches,
load them
into burlap sacks
ready to take
to the oil press.

At the end of the day
Costas unveils a bottle of wine
and three small glasses.

We raise a toast to the harvest.

Στην υγειά σας!
(Stin ygeiá sas!)
To our health!

We take a sip.

When can I help you
finish your boat, brother?

A smile spreads
across my sister's face
as wide
as the Aegean Sea.

Soldiers have entered our village

I am worried for our safety.

They sit in the square and drink
strong coffee
and cloudy ouzo.

Their rifles
resting on the table.

They think they are here
to protect us.

The captain watches
the young girls
at the fountain.

The hungry eyes
of a wolf
who has been
trained to hunt.

No goat, no milk

no feta.

Prices are soaring.
The stores have no bread.

Our village is hungry.

I feel the desperation
and anger
bubbling up.

A kettle
held over a flame.

I take our donkey

and follow the switchback trails
down to the shore.

Maliakos Kolpos, our green-blue
bay, wrapped by a belt
of land.

The fishermen dock their boats.
They empty their nets.

Hundreds of silver fish,
alive and thrashing,
spill onto the dock.

We sort the fish by size,
toss them into wicker baskets.

I load them onto the donkey.

The baskets hang
from my trusted friend
who will heft my load
through the steep hills.

The fishmongers wait
in the village square.

The women
push and elbow each other
to snatch the best catch
of the day.

They take the silver bodies
in both hands
and inhale deeply.

The smell of the sea clings
to the glinting scales.

The fishmongers pay
three salted fish
and a few coins
for my help.

Someday, I swear,
I will not be a boy on a donkey.
I will be a man in a boat.

As I walk home through the dust

I think about
my unfinished boat,
my *kaiki.*

It will be
my donkey
of the sea.

Reliable
and sturdy.

Good
in all weather.

Whatever
Poseidon
sends my way.

I don't need
a sleek, fast
boat.

I say to myself,

It is better
to get to where
you are going

than to rush
and never
get there at all.[12]

The trail is lined with almond trees

and cedar.

I take the air
into my nose and mouth,
breathe the deep scent
of the hills.

Down the path,
I hear men laughing.

Then I hear someone scream.

A group of soldiers
has circled a girl
from our village.

Her dress is torn
and one of her braids
has come loose.

There is a red ribbon
on the ground.

She looks at me
with eyes that say,
Help me.

I break through the circle
and scold her.
Mariana! Your mother is looking for you!

One of the soldiers smirks
and with a high-pitched voice
he teases,
Mariana, your mama is calling!

He lifts the back of her skirt
with the tip of his gun
as I pull her
away from the men.

I swing my leg
over the donkey's back
and lift her up.

Wrap my arm
tightly
around her waist
and nudge my heel
sharply
into the donkey's belly.

I look back
and see the soldier laughing.

The gun
still in his hand.

The next day

Violetta bounds
through the doorway.

Her cheeks are rosy
and her eyes are wide.

What is it?
Is something wrong?
I ask.

There is a knife
in my stomach
trying to come
out of my throat.

I will kill
if someone has hurt her.

Oh Gio, she says
as a shy smile rises
on the corner
of her lips.

She grabs my hands.
I'm going to have a baby.

Jeanne

We ride the train

A pilgrimage
to Mont Saint-Michel.

The sacred cathedral
at the top of the hill.

It rises,
isolated on its own island
in the middle
of miles of salt marsh.

My mother wants to pray
for my father's
safe return.

After we arrive
at the train station,
we begin to walk.

We see the mount
far ahead,
swallowed by the mouth
of the Couesnon river.

We must wait
for the tides to retreat.

We wait until it is safe.

We bare our feet
to the soft wet silt
of the channel.

Each step takes us closer
to the sacred island
cathedral.

Outside the walls
of the commune
the fishermen and farmers
motion and yell for pilgrims
to buy their goods.

We walk through
the barricade.

A drawbridge,
with a large wooden door,
so heavy
it looks like
it could protect the cathedral
from an army of giants.

The streets spiral upward
to the stone ramparts.

I stand
and look out
at the miles of sand
and watch
the tide come in
as swiftly
as a galloping horse. [13]

Inside the church

I light a candle
at the altar
of Jeanne d'Arc.

My namesake.

She stands tall and proud,
a warrior,
like a man.

She felt the love
of the spirit

when she rode
on the back of her horse
with her banner
flying

and also
in the heart
of the fire.

I have always felt

the spirit.

It begins with a tingle
then my body feels warm.

It's like opening up a dam
in a river
and then everything
rushes through—
all emotion
all love
all.

Sometimes,
I feel it
in a church
and sometimes
I don't.

I always feel it
when I stare at trees
moving in the wind.

And when I hear music.

Today, kneeling
beside my mother
in the most beautiful church
in the world

I ask this Great Spirit,

*Please,
bring my father home.*

Letter #7

October 21, 1918

How could the stars have brought us together?

We were born so far apart. Separated by culture, language, and land, and yet we found each other.

Yours always and forever,
Loup

I convince

Elena and Marguerite
to go on an adventure
after school.

American Coney Island?

> *I just want to try
> something different.*

We see the red,
white, and blue sign
from down the block.

An American eagle
waves us in.

Billy is seated
at a table with his back to the door.

He looks scrubbed and clean.

Surrounded by men
of all different colors
with grease on their faces.

Men, who have been working
on the factory floor all day.

> *Let's sit over here.*

I lead the girls to a table
in the connecting room
away from Billy.

We don't have money for food,
so we order colas.

Heading to the bathroom,

I say, gripping my middle.

Are you ok?

Marguerite looks concerned.

You're acting weird.

I'm fine. I'll be right back.

I sit down

next to Billy.

His face lights up
when he sees me.

I was afraid you wouldn't show.
I got this for you.

He slides
a chocolate malt
toward me.

I smile
and take a long pull
from the straw.

Close my eyes.

It's the first time
I've ever tasted ice cream.

Tell me about yourself

I laugh.
>My name is Mary.

Mary, Mary, quite contrary?

>My parents
>wouldn't disagree with you.

Why?

>We don't want
>the same things.

*Tell me
what you want.*

>What do I want?

Yes.
>You mean, like a hamburger?

*No.
What do you want
from life?*

I hesitate.

No one
has ever asked me
what I want.

>I want to work.

What kind of work?

>Own a business
>like my father.

I know that's unusual
for a woman.

Maybe impossible.

Don't you want
to have
a husband
and babies?

Can't I have both?

I hold my breath.

I guess you don't know
until you try.

And you?

I place my palms
on the table and lean in.

What do you want?

He takes a sip from his straw.

With a shy smile
he responds,

     You.

I choke on my chocolate shake.

*How could you
possibly know
you want me?*

You just met me!

     You're beautiful.

Thank you.

I'm blushing.

     *You're interesting.
Different.*

*Isn't that a polite way
of saying I'm odd?*

     *I've never met
anyone else
whose eyes change color.*

I put my hands
over my eyes.

I thought
they only turned bright green
when I was angry!

> *Holy moly!*
> *Bright green.*
> *I can't wait!*

Yes, you can.

> *They also turn*
> *turquoise*
> *when you're excited.*

> *Gray, when you're calm.*

> *The color of olives*
> *when you feel . . . friendly?*

> *That's all*
> *I've noticed so far.*

I've only been told
what they look like
when I'm angry.

Why hasn't
anyone in my family
noticed
all the colors
that I feel?

You have a very fancy car

I blurt out
and then feel embarrassed.

> Yes.

> It's a bit much.

Do you work?

> I'm in school.
> Sales and marketing.

> A job lined up
> with Ford
> when I graduate.

> My father
> got me the job.

He looks annoyed and then says,

> He imagines
> I am incapable
> of accomplishing
> important tasks
> without him.

Fathers.
They imagine they know us.
But they don't, do they?

> Not in the least.

Then he asks the question

I've been waiting for.

Are you Greek?

> *My father is Greek.*
> *My mother is French.*

> *I am American.*

I shrink
into my dress.

I would rather
discuss
a contagious rash
than discuss
my parents.

He smiles and says,
When I was seven,
my uncle gave me a book
on Greek mythology.

I was obsessed.

I thought about the gods
and Mount Olympus
all the time.

I tried to imagine
who everyone would be
if they were a god.

I think I'd be Apollo.
I love the sun, music, and poetry.

I was just
sitting here wondering
who you would be.

I think you would be
Athena.

She's strong, like you.

I want to tell him

I am not as strong
as he thinks I am.

I want to tell him

about Dimitris.

My father's plans.

The promises
that have been made.

I want to tell him

about his eyes.

They never change.
Steady.
Pure blue.

I want to tell him

we can't
see each other again.

I want to tell him

I must be
a *Good Greek Girl.*

But I don't.

I let the sweet
coldness
of my chocolate shake
swirl around
the inside of my skull.

It makes my head hurt.

Makes me forget
everything.

Except for his hand
on mine.

I hear someone

clearing their throat.

I turn to see Marguerite,
arms crossed.

Glaring at me.

Call me Athena

She wasn't
a *Good Greek Girl*
either.

Athena, why do you fight?

Put down your sword and shield
and make your bed.

Athena, come down from your chariot,
take off your golden helmet,
and come to dinner.

Athena, did you injure your father
when you leapt from his head?

Why can't you be more like Aphrodite?
She's pretty and polite
and she knows how to entertain.

Athena, please stop thinking
you are the queen of Athens.

You're only a girl from Detroit.

Giorgos (Gio)

Faster than a sail

swells with wind,
my sister's belly
becomes round
with life.

My mother dotes on her.

Put your feet up, Violetta!
Don't carry that, Violetta!

One day
my sister snatches my hand
and presses my palm
into her hard stomach.

Costas laughs
as my mouth drops open.

So many swirling movements
up and down
like a ship
cresting on a wave.

My sister closes her eyes
and sighs.

I wonder
what it feels like
to hold the ocean
inside.

Costas tries to sell olive oil

from his groves,
but the prices have dropped.

I grab his arm.

We need to do something.
Violetta is hungry.
I'm worried
soon she will be
too weak.

We eat what we can grow
in our garden:
figs and tomatoes,
lettuce,
and beans.

We have
no meat
no cheese
no flour
no bread.

Violetta's cheeks are hollow.

I walk in the village after dark.

The sweet pink oleander
smells like apricots.

My stomach is as empty
as my coin purse.

I love my sister

I want her to live.

Costas and I
sneak into the hills
and find a lamb
that is fat enough.

After the killing,
Costas hoists the body
onto his shoulder.

The legs wrap around his neck
like a scarf.

We do not feel happy.

We have done
what was needed.

We are almost home
when a group of men
come running up the path.

Stop! Thieves!

One of the men
pulls out a long rifle.

He aims.

Costas turns and screams:
Run, Giorgos, run.

The bullet connects
with his head.

Costas looks stunned for a moment,
his expression frozen in silence

and then his body falls
to the ground.

Jeanne

Maman says I should

be happy.

I get to go to school.

When she was young,
they didn't allow girls to study.

I love the smell of chalk
and old books that are foxed
around the edges.

I wash my black slate
and dust my desk.

I learn to write sentences
and solve number problems.

After lunch,
we put our heads on our desks
and our teacher reads to us.

The rhythm of her voice
whirls around us like sea air.

She's really very bright,
the teacher tells my mother
after school.
*Maybe someday she'll be a doctor,
like her father.*

My eyes open wide.
I clasp my hands
in front of my heart.

Maman wipes her eyes
with a handkerchief.

Yes. Maybe. Someday.

Of course, I dream

of being a doctor.

No one else in town
thinks
it's an appropriate job
for a girl.

I will prove
them wrong.

Papa says I can do it.

I can change
people's minds
like Madame Curie.

I imagine
my long, black dress
covered
in a lab coat.

Leaning over
petri dishes, glass vials,
beakers,
and Bunsen burners.

After I make
my grand discoveries
I will stand on the stage
in Stockholm.

A Nobel Prize in my hand.

My aunt

Sister Marie-Thérèse
joins us for lunch.

I ask my mother
to serve her favorite meal:
roasted lamb
with new potatoes
and asparagus.

My aunt
is the mother superior
at the Abbaye Notre-Dame
de Saint-Malo.

She manages
Les Filles de la Sagesse,
the sisters of the convent
and the hospital
where they work
with wounded soldiers
arriving from the front.

I wait through the entire meal.
I try to breathe slowly.

I even let her take two bites
of her flaky, buttery
Kouign-amann
before I ask
if it would be possible
to volunteer at the hospital
two days a week after school.

She takes her napkin
and delicately pats
the corners of her mouth.

I hold my breath.

You're sixteen now.
I don't see why not.

I look at my mother.

She smiles and pats
my trembling hand.

Letter #8

October 25, 1918

Let us start a life together.

Build something new.

Find joy.

A place of peace in this war-torn world.

Yours always,
Petit Oiseau

Billy circles around me

both hands
above
the handlebars.

I can't help
but tease him.

You look like
a circus performer!

He slows the bicycle,
balances on his left foot,
swings his right leg
over the bar,
and trots alongside.

An acrobat
hopping
on and off
a trained
white horse.

    You should try it.

I bet you think I won't.

    Oh, I know you won't.
    You're chicken.

He flashes
a daring smile.

The hairs
on back of my neck
stand straight.

Hold this for me, sister.

I shove
my stack of books
into Marguerite's
arms.

   Mary, no!

Marguerite,
do we really
have to be good
all the time?

I mount the metal beast

My skirt is in the way.

I tie the extra fabric
in a knot
exposing my legs.

Marguerite gasps.

I place both feet
on the pedals.

As awkward
as a bear on a bicycle.

In a moment
of quick defeat
I tumble
to one side.

You gotta move
before you start pedaling.
Let me help you.

Billy puts one hand
on the handlebars
and one hand on the seat.

His entire body
touches mine.

Electricity
runs up my spine.

He begins to push me.

Pedal, Mary, pedal!

I force my legs up and down.
Push and pump.

Billy runs beside me.

A tuft of wind
escape his lips
as he gives the bicycle
a mighty shove

I am
wheeling and turning
spinning.

Under the big top,
on my own.

I feel elated

all the way home.

Marguerite,
you can't imagine
how it feels!

Like you're flying!

She smiles a half-smile,
but I know
she's concerned.

Have I embarrassed her?
Is she ashamed of me?

What?

My sister
won't look at me.

She takes a big breath
and finally says,

I saw John
in the square.

He's going to tell
father.

My father slaps me

My head whips sideways.

The imprint of his hand
blooms
on my cheek.

Why?

I brush the hair
out of my eyes.

Stare him down
hard
with my green eyes
so that he cannot
hold
my gaze.

*It was only a ride
on a bicycle.*

> *I am your father.
> I need to protect you!*

> *From others and yourself!*

> *I know what can happen.
> I have seen . . .*

He stops,
unable to complete
his sentence.

> *It is my duty
> to make sure you are safe.*

I can see us both from above.

A father
who is afraid
for his child.

A daughter
who is beyond saving.

Call me Athena

The girl
who should have been born
a boy.

I wake, and it's warm

and sticky beneath me.

I think
I've wet the bed,
then I realize
I'm bleeding.

The emotions
of the night before
grip my insides,
wring them
like a sheet.

Everything
in my life
seems harder
than usual.

Even the wild things
that cannot
be controlled.

I roll Marguerite
to the other side
of the bed
and peel the covering.

I wish I could
hide the soiled cloth,
my shame.

There's no hiding
in our tiny
apartment.

My mother's face
at the door.

My mother heats three kettles

Pours the boiling liquid
into the porcelain bath.

Mixes
water from the tap
until it is steaming
and warm.

I enter slowly.
Settle down
into the deep.

The water turns pink.

I shed a month
of pain.

My mother leans
my head back
pours water
over my unruly hair
and says,

*Someday, you will love your body
and the way it works.*

*It is miraculous.
It can grow a child.*

She lathers soap
and pours another pitcher
over my head.

I close my eyes
and imagine her saying,

Then you will understand suffering.

I know I was wrong

*I shouldn't
have ridden a bicycle.*

My mother clears
her throat.

> *And?*

*I shouldn't
have ridden a boy's
bicycle
because it sends
the wrong message.*

> *And?*

And I won't do it again.

*But it makes me
so angry
that John told Father!*

My mother
looks at me.

She kisses my forehead.

> *It wasn't John.*

How could she?

My sister.
My twin.

Weren't we
once
radios
tuned to the same
frequency?

Now, I feel
my dial
spinning.

I cannot find her.

Giorgos (Gio)

Everything is breath, everything is heartbeat

I run as fast as I can.

I hear men shouting and dogs barking.

Do you see him? Where did he go?

I know this land.

I find the opening of the cave
where Violetta and I used to explore.

Don't breathe. Don't move.

I wait.

Stay hidden. Stay silent.

Even after
the sound of the dogs
and the men are gone

my heart beats like a battle drum.

I follow the shadows home

my steps
soft and light.

I hide in the
bushes

check to make sure
no one
sees me.

A barn owl calls out
a warning
as I enter our yard.

I see my unfinished
kaiki.

The smooth boards
that I have sanded
for hours.

I do not have
the wood and resin
I need
to finish the hull.

Without it
I will not be able
to navigate
across the water.

My mother is asleep

in her bed.

My heart aches
at the thought
of saying goodbye.

I sneak around the house,
try not to wake her.

Find a sack
and stuff it with figs and tomatoes,
then fill a sheep's bladder
with water.

Pack matches
and a warm sweater.

Roll a thin wool blanket
and tie it to my sack.

If I don't leave now,
I will go to prison.

I open the door
of my childhood home.

My mother rises.

From her face,
I know that the men from the village
have told her.

I cannot open my mouth
to say goodbye.

She holds my shoulders
as tears stream down my face.

Finally, she looks me in my eyes
with love, sharp as
an eagle's talon.

Go, my child,
and never come back.

In a blur

of hunger and pain,

I climb onto
the donkey's back
and lean my face
into its hide.

The sky is filled with indigo light.

I fall asleep
to the rhythm
of the hooves
hitting the dirt path.

With a jolt,
the donkey stops.

I lay my blanket down
in a field.

The dry grass
slices into my back.

My cheeks are burning.
My mouth dry.

Over and over,
I see Costas fall.

I hear my sister weeping.

Jeanne

Madame Leroux

inspects
our starched
white uniforms.

She leads us
through
l'hopital du Rosais,
instructing us
with a crisp,
clear voice.

I feel confident
until we reach
the surgical unit
where the air is thick
with blood
and pus-soaked
bandages.

We hesitate at the door
and see a doctor
sawing the leg
of a screaming
soldier.

I grab my stomach
and vomit
into the closest
bedpan.

Leroux points to the pan

Around the corner
to the right.

Bring it back, clean.

I run down the hall
and locate
the metal hatch
for the incinerator.

I empty the pan
quickly
into the fire
below.

The smell catches me.
I'm going
to be sick again.

I wipe my brow
and bump into a soldier
on a gurney.

Help me,
he whispers.

He grabs me,
trembling,
his hands covered
in blood.

Please.
Please.

He closes his eyes,
his breath labored.
He places his palm
on his breast pocket.

Please.

I find a small
photograph.

A woman
with light eyes
and yellow curls.

Eyes full of love.

I wipe the blood
onto my apron
and place the frame
in his hand.

Who is she?
I ask.

His eyes
stare straight ahead.

The picture
has fallen
out of his hand.

My new
white uniform
stained red. [14]

What did you learn today?

my mother asks me

as our maid, Anne,
ladles creamy asparagus soup
into a china bowl.

She places a shiny silver spoon
on my napkin
and lays a plump cut
of roast beef
dripping
with sauce
onto a plate.

What should I say to her?

Can I describe
the wounds from the mustard gas,
the bubbled skin,
the yellow eyes?

The sound of more
than one
wounded soldier
screaming for help?

It is only
a twenty-minute walk
from my house
to the hospital.

The difference
between them
makes me feel
like I have traveled
many hours.

Between
the land of plenty
and the land
of the forgotten.

Letter #9

October 27, 1918

I wish I could feed every starving child I see.

I do not have enough to give.

I pray for a time of peace and sustenance—when families can keep the wheat they grow and children can, once again, grow plump from their mother's milk.

I am done with the ways of men and the suffering that comes with war.

Yours forever,
Loup

I take the trash

to the alleyway behind the store.

I hear crying.

Peeling paint.
Gray stone.

The wind is howling,
an alley cat
scratching its back
on the iron rods
of barred windows
and gated doors.

I hear something
whimpering.

Look around
and see no living
creature.

The wind lifts
the tips of newspapers
strewn across
the muddy lane.

They flap in a rhythm.

I follow the sound
to the street.

I see a large basket
filled with laundry
tucked into
a storefront.

A small foot
pushes out
of the white
cloth.

I dig into the basket

gingerly
with two fingers.

It's an infant.

Lips blue.

There is a note
attached to her dress.

Please,
help my child.

I have no money
to support her.

Forgive me.

The child emits
a terrible screech.

Hunger.

I unbutton my coat
and my dress.

I press the child
to my skin
for warmth.

She opens her mouth
sucks hard
on my neck.

Milk.

She breathes
in shallow
spasms.

I have nothing
to give her.

Help!

I tuck the child
into the basket
and begin to run
toward
the firehouse.

I see a woman
pushing a pram with a tiny infant
tucked warm inside.

Please!
This baby is starving!

She looks at me
like I am vermin.

What am I supposed to do about it?

She walks on.

Please! Help!
She'll die!

I look around the square
for another adult.

My desperation
growing.

I feel someone pull me
from behind.

I turn and see a young woman
dressed in clean clothes.

Her blond hair
a glowing lantern
against
the gray stones.

I have an infant at home.
She takes the child
from me.

I can help you.

She sits on a stoop
shielded from the street
behind a low bush.

She wraps
the blanket around her
like a shawl
and holds
the infant to her.

The child latches.

I hear
famished
frantic
gulping.

Shhhhh.
There.
Shhhhhh.

I look away,
overwhelmed
with emotion.

Someday,
I pray, I will grow
into the kind
of woman
who will give
everything she can
to a child in need.

My name is Lara

she says and smiles.

We walk to
to Sacred Heart Church
around the corner.

Weave through
the lines of people
waiting for food
and donations.

This is my church.
I know they will help,
Lara says.

She finds a nun,
who leads us
to a white-collared
priest.

His eyes drop
with pity
and sadness.

He embraces the child
and disappears
into the crowd.

Lara and I

hesitate
outside of the church.

Our arms feel empty.

Throngs of people waiting
in line to be fed.

Well, don't just stand there.
Grab a ladle and help!

A woman,
wearing an apron
decorated with huge red flowers,
hands me
a giant spoon.

I don't work here.

You do now!

She pushes us
behind the table.

That's the problem
with doing one good deed.

You get roped into another.

Her round belly jiggles
when she chuckles.

I'm Clarabelle.

I'm in charge
of charitable donations
at the church.

She tells Lara
to tear chunks of bread.

Place them
on the side of the bowls
I'm filling
with thin
vegetable soup.

We feed the homeless drifters.

Mostly men
with dirt under
their nails
and mud
on their boots.

Finally, a mother
and her three
children.

Her oldest daughter
drops to her hands and knees,
crawls under the table
to kiss my feet.

After an hour

I excuse myself.

Clarabelle
shakes my hand
and thanks me
for my help.

Her red-flowered apron
soaked
with sloshed broth.

Come back next week
for the clothing drive!

We could use
all the hands we can get.

> *I'll be there.*
> *You should come!*

Lara says,
as she squeezes me
into a hug.

Walking home,
I pass by the shop window
with the emerald-green dress
that I will never own.

I see women
strolling down
the avenue.

Fur coats flow
around their ankles.

Necks wrapped
in knotted strings
of pearls
and beaded scarves.

The parade of hungry
hollow faces
still sharp
in my mind.

Grateful

for my family

and the simple meal

waiting for me

at home.

Giorgos (Gio)

KOMNINA, CENTRAL GREECE
1917

I dream of the gods

of my ancestors.

Superhumans
who swoop down
from Mount Olympus
on swift chariots
pulled by powerful horses.

They know I am suffering.

The gods of wine and beauty,
the harvest, and the sea.

I pray they will help me.

Shower me with
bolts of lightning
that will pierce the heart
of anyone
who wishes harm.

But I am afraid,
that the ancient immortals
have vanished.

And we are left with one god,
who has turned his back
on me.

I sell the donkey

to a fat farmer
for almost nothing
and hitch a ride
on a horse-drawn cart
on its way
to Athens.

The miles
rattle through my bones.

When we get closer
to the city,
I see the ruins
of the Acropolis
poised high
on a limestone bluff.

Bright-blue sky
peers through
the gleaming white columns
of the Parthenon.

I feel the power of the stone
pulse into me.

We weave south
through the streets
of Athens
heading to
the Port of Piraeus.

The harbor looks like
the gates of hell.

Factories fill the skyline.
Smokestacks cough
black sludge.

A huge steamship
looms above
like a mountain
of welded steel.

I have always known.

I have to get on that ship.

The farmer slows

and I hop off
while the wagon
is still moving.

I run at a full sprint.

I hear the whistle blow
and push my legs farther.

Don't leave.
Don't leave without me.

Hundreds of passengers
swarm the gangplank,
pushing and shoving to get on.

I get close and watch
a small boy drop his toy.

I crouch next to the child
and talk to him in a soothing voice
like a brother or a friend.

The parents
hand their bundle of tickets
to the attendant.

I walk up the plank
behind them.

There is a crowd on the deck

I blend into the gray jackets
and caps of the gentlemen,
the swirling chaos
of luggage and limbs.

I listen for shouting.
Wait for a hand on my collar.

No one comes.

I resist the need
to drop to my knees
in exhaustion
and relief.

I lean against the railing
and hear the rattling
of a heavy chain.

Feel the anchor lift.

My boat
steers toward
the open sea.

Jeanne

We don't hear exact

numbers.

We just hear the words
full train.

We know
there will be hundreds
on stretchers,
caked
in dried mud.

I help
the walking wounded
to their beds.

Cut the bloody
shreds of uniform
from their bodies.

Wash their limbs
and faces,
black and pocked
with gun smoke
and shrapnel.

They chatter to themselves.
Nonsensical
strings of words.

Names of boys
who were wounded,
boys
who were left
behind.

Where is . . . fallen . . .
now . . . gone . . . help . . .

Wounds
crawling with maggots.

Stinking and tense
with gangrene.

One boy
won't stop screaming.

For a moment
I think,
He will drive us all mad.

And then I hate myself.

One poor lad,
eyes shot through,
calmly asks me,
Shall I need a surgery?
I can't see.

I cannot bring myself
to tell him,
Poor boy.
You will never see again. [14, 15]

Death walks the halls

a feeling, a smell.

It lures
the last oxygen
from lungs.

Coughs out
promises
of freedom.

Through the window,
past the city gates
to the deep waters
below.

Death walks the halls

naked,
without pride,
asking for his mother.

He is angry.
He is blind.
He is shameful
and alone.

Death walks the halls

not as a cloaked
demon
but as a nurse
with a clipboard

who closes
a young boy's eyes
and marks the time
his heart
stopped beating.

Death walks the halls

as a child

with his pockets
full of tin soldiers

his eyes wide open,
his head full
of dreams.

Death walks the halls

as a doctor

who says
to the mothers and the fathers

There was nothing more
we could
do.

Letter #10

October 29, 1918

The weather turned today.

I wrapped myself in a shawl and stood at the doorway and watched the first snow.

There among the crystals and cold, I saw lilting white wings flying higher, the opposite direction as the falling flakes.

It was a snow-white moth. Trying its hardest to fight the frost.

Yours,
Petit Oiseau

Mrs. Patterson lectures

about the Ford Hunger March.

My class
leans forward.

We rest our chins
on our knuckles
and listen closely.

One year ago,

six thousand men marched
from downtown Detroit
to the River Rouge factory.

Sixty men were wounded
and four were killed
on that day.

Dearborn streets were littered
with broken glass and
automobile wreckage.

Nearly every window
in the Ford plant
broken. [16]

Elena's father was there

He sits on a stool
at the front of the classroom.

Tells us of the men
who marched against
the bitter wind
on March 7, 1932.

The Ford Massacre.

We marched
from Detroit
to the River Rouge Plant
with demands
for Henry Ford.

We held signs that read,

"Give us Work"
"We Want Bread Not Crumbs"
"Tax the Rich and Feed the Poor"

As we got closer
to the plant,
Ford's hired goons
attacked us.

Tear gas, fire hoses,
clubs.

Men running everywhere
trying to escape
the bullets
pelting the crowd.

A boy was shot.

Blood spread
across his chest
like a car dripping oil
onto the pavement.

They called us REDS.

All we wanted was health care
and an end
to racial discrimination.

Elena's father
pauses,
wipes his face
and eyes
with a handkerchief.

The next day,
many men
dressed in their uniforms
and went to the factory.

Stepped over
red stains
on the sidewalk.

Black,
where the fires had burned.

Men with work
don't dare complain
about conditions. [16]

The chalk squeaks

as Mrs. Patterson writes
our shared history
on the blackboard.

In 1929—Detroit produced 5,337,000 vehicles.

October 24, 1929—the stock market crashed.

In 1930—3,363,000 vehicles

In 1931—1,332,000 vehicles[17]

Fewer vehicles = fewer jobs

Current 1933 unemployment rate = 26% and rising.[18]

She doesn't
have to tell us
about the unemployed.

We've all seen the families
waiting for bread
outside of Sacred Heart.

The violence
that comes from desperation.

The clash between
those who have
and those who don't.

I remember the parade

on March 12, 1932.

We gathered together
as a community.

Sixty thousand strong.

Marched down
Woodward Avenue
past the Institute of Arts,
then turned west
to the Woodmere Cemetery.

Workers and families
singing songs of revolution.

Grieving
for the dead.

The cemetery refused
Curtis Williams
because of the color of his skin.

Airplanes scattered
his ashes
over River Rouge.

No Ford
or Dearborn officials
were prosecuted for
the deaths. [19]

My father held my hand,
worried I would be lost
in the crowd.

He held me tighter
when we saw
a safety commission officer
shove his gun
into the face
of one of the workers.

We put four
of your kind into the graves
with this.

And we'll put a lot more
if we have to. [16]

On our way home from school

Billy's red
convertible
glides up
beside us.

Do you want a lift?

I look at my sister.

She shakes her head
vehemently
and holds up her hands.

Come on, Mary!

She starts walking
quickly.

I lag behind.

Billy drives slowly
right next to me.

*There's a big band playing
at the Bob-Lo Island Pavilion
on Sunday night.*

I'd like to take you.

*We could take the ferry to Belle Isle.
Walk the promenade.*

> *Billy,
> you know I can't.*

*If you're going to talk to me that way,
you'd better call me William.*

That's what my mother calls me
when she's telling me "no."

     My father would kill me.

Come on, Mary!
It'll be fun.

     You know I can't.

The real question is:
do you have "the jitters."

I laugh.

I've only heard
that phrase
on the radio.

     Some say there's too much
     "jitter in my jitterbug." [20]

Great.
It's settled.

I'll see you at the dock
at 4:30 on Sunday.

He flashes me
a toothy grin,
presses his foot to the gas.

Glides
down the road
before I can say,

*Good Greek Girls
don't jitterbug.*

My father paces around the store

I look at the books.

We haven't had a customer
in hours.

I see the red numbers
floating at the bottom
of the page.

*There's more money going out
than coming in.*

*I'm going to have to cancel
the shipments.*

My father avoids my eyes.

>*What can we do?*

I ask,
feeling optimistic.

>*Can we advertise?*
>*Can we create a sale?*

It won't help.

>*You don't know that, Baba!*
>*We just have to try some new things!*

The banks have failed.
Less cars are being made.
The food lines are getting longer.
People are living on the street.

No one has money to spend
on colas and cream.

I walk around the counter
to stand next to my father.

We're going to lose the business, Mary.

Now, I know.

Why he is pushing me
to marry Dimitris.

Giorgos (Gio)

ATLANTIC OCEAN
1917

On a bench, beneath the stars

Sister, see me.

Poised on the edge
of the earth

hovering between
the black
of the ocean
and sky.

Sister, hear me.

I wish
I could throw a hatchet
into the heavens

tear a hole
in the gut of the past.

Sister, forgive me.

My rage, my guilt,
my fear.

I am to blame.

I know the cries
of a fatherless son.

I surrender my grief

to the Furies.

Three sisters
with snakes in their hair
coal-black bodies
bat wings
bloodred eyes.

I imagine
the mythical crones
rip into my flesh,
punish me
with their claws.

I try to brush them away,
but I know
I will never be free.

As they whisper and hiss
into my ear,

Do not dream, young one.

You will never return
to your homeland.

I roam the deck during the day

No one suspects me.

When night falls,
I hide in the engine room,
cover my ears,
try to block the sound
of the massive
whirling pistons
and the rumble
of the turbine.

I crouch
in the coal bunkers,
calf-deep in oily water.

There are a few
other stowaways.

Most of them boys
my age.

For nine days
we help each other.

Steal food off plates and share.

I can't decide
what I fear most.

Another night on this ship
or what will happen
when we finally
arrive.

My body jerks

awake
with the sound of a whistle.

My muscles tense
and eardrums bulge
with alarm.

There is a man
looming over
our sleeping bodies,
shouting,

Stowaways!

Jeanne

Most of the nurses

have fiancés, brothers,
and fathers
in the war.

We throw ourselves
into our duties.

Transform our
worry and sadness
into healing.

All of these boys
coming from the front lines
are someone's fiancé,
someone's son.

We treat each soldier
like family.

Some days, it is difficult
to remember

that these boys
are not ours.

When the soldiers

are homesick,
I write letters
to their mothers and wives.

When they are bored,
I read them poetry
and novels
about romance
and spies.

When they cannot speak,
I hold their hands.

When they are lonely,
I sing Breton folksongs
in Gaelic.

When they need a friend,
I tell them about Papa
and his bravery.

I let them call me
petit oiseau.

Nurses arrive

from Great Britain
and the United States
by train and by boat.

They have come to help
the French people
and also the soldiers
from their homelands.

I am learning
to speak English
more each day
and I am teaching them
to say little phrases
in French.

We laugh at the
faux amis.

Words that sound
the same
but mean
something else.

Brasserie and *brassiere* (bra);
blessed and *blessé* (injured);
coin and *coin* (corner).

Speaking a new language
is like wearing a new
pair of glasses.

My new friend Vera

hands me a cup of tea
and leads me outside.

It's a lovely day
and the roses are blooming.

Vera is blond and beautiful.

A shined-up penny
in a pocketful
of dull coins.

She's from Indiana.

She tells me about
her family and their house
and their land
where they grow
miles of corn.

Her town
used to be all farmland,
but now
there are a lot of buildings
in the center.

They have concerts
with brass bands
and parades on holidays
and they sit on the curb
and drink Coca-Cola
and watch
the decorated trucks
drive past
the crowds.

She tells me
that right before she left,
her town got a stoplight.

When they installed it,
people stood on the corner
and watched the light
change from red
to green to yellow
for hours.

Then she gives a little
snort-laugh
like a pink piglet.

It's not much, but it's my home!

She also tells me
about the big, modern
American cities
with the tallest buildings
in the whole world.

I stare at the
two-story
buildings
that line the streets
of Saint-Malo.

I decide
someday I would like
to see buildings
that scrape
the sky.

Letter #11

October 30, 1918

Yesterday, I found a ribbon lying on the ground—abandoned in a field.

So blue against the green grass and brown earth.

I picked it up and felt the soft silk.

Wished that I could tie it in your hair.

Forever yours,
Loup

A group

of women and girls gather
to help with the clothing drive
at Sacred Heart.

Mary!
I'm so glad you made it!

Clarabelle's cheeks
are shiny with sweat.

Her red-flowered
apron tied around
her plump waist.

I have the perfect job for you!

She takes me to a room
filled to the brim
with donations.

People have been
dropping things off
all day.

We need help sorting it.

Several women
look up from their work
to wave hello.

I see Lara.

She hops up
and gives me a hug.

Clarabelle continues,

Please make piles:
men's shirts
pants
women's dresses
sweaters
belts.

You get the drift.

She picks up a pair of pants
and points at a tear.

If there's something
to mend,
bring it to me.

I have a sewing machine.

Oh, and don't forget
to check the pockets.

She tosses the pants into a pile.

Last month,
a man
received a loaf of bread
and a white
button-down shirt.

The next day he returned.

There were diamond cufflinks
still attached to the sleeves. [17]

She chuckles
and pats my shoulder.

I tell you, honesty
is still alive
in America.

Although, I think
those diamond cufflinks
went directly
into the church
donation box,
she says with a grin.

To entertain ourselves

we turn on the wireless,
and a crackled voice
whines through the speakers.

*Wearing a white silk gown
and white gloves,*

*Earhart broke up a dinner at the White House
by inviting the first lady
on a flight to Baltimore
and back.*

*Earhart was at the controls
of the plane
most of the flight.*

*Amelia Earhart
and the first lady!*

Lara grabs my arm.

*A match
made in heaven!*

I squeal.

We lean in to listen
as Eleanor Roosevelt's voice
floats over the airwaves.

*I'd love to do it myself.
I make no bones about it.*

*It does mark an epoch,
doesn't it,
when a girl in an evening dress
and slippers*

can pilot a plane
at night. [21]

We both smile,
eyes full of joy and light.

A sunrise, a blessing,
a wide open
horizon.

I spend the next few hours thinking

about flying alone in a plane

while digging my way
through a pile
of random junk.

Some of it
makes me smile.

Some makes me
gag.

I find an itchy pair
of woolen pants
with a pair of soiled underwear
still attached.

A hat
with an entire pheasant,
its teal and rust
wing
stretched
across the brim.

Plastic waders
for fishing in deep water.

A brassiere
with padded cups
as large
as two elephant feet.

I hold it up to my body
and dance.

Lara starts giggling.

She puts on
a pair of Coke-bottle glasses
and pretends to use
a pair of dentures.

The other girls go bananas.

At the very end of the day

I see something
peeking out
from a pile of gray.

A swath
of emerald green
silk.

I pull

and pull and pull
and it keeps coming
like a silk scarf
being pulled
out of
a magic hat.

It's an evening dress

Sleeveless,
bias-cut, and soft
as the inside
of a rabbit's ear.

It must have been
worn once.

It's perfect

except for a tear
running
all the way down
the seam.

I bring the dress to Clarabelle

secretly
hoping she'll
think it's unfixable
and throw it
away.

Instead she takes it,
turns it inside out,
and runs it through
the sewing machine.

The needle
bobs efficiently along
the silky fabric
like she's mending
a muslin
housedress.

That'll probably do.

Now that I look at it,
it's about your size, Mary.

Will you try it on
so I can see if
it needs any other mending?

I try to contain my excitement
as I duck
behind a changing screen.

Slip my legs through
the glossy fabric.

Come out
and present myself.

She looks at me
with a pained expression.

Oh, Mary.

      What's wrong?

It looks like it was meant for you.

She lifts the zipper
and turns me
toward the mirror.

All the other volunteers
gather to look.

I look at myself
in the mirror,
covered in soft green silk.

The color
bounces off my dark hair
and light eyes.

I've never felt
so beautiful.

You must take it home!

One of the women says.

What shoe size are you, Mary?
Will these fit?

Lara hands me
a pair of
silver T-strap high heels.

I slip my heel
into them
and they fit.

Ooooo! What about this?

Yet another volunteer
rummages
through her piles
and produces
a silver and pearl hairpin
in the shape of a star.

And this!

Another woman
produces a silvery ribbon.
Pins the star to it
and strings it
though my black, curly hair.

I couldn't possibly
take all this.

I've never worn
anything this nice.

I stare in the mirror.
Could this really be me?

Clarabelle hugs me tight

around my shoulders.

Consider it a thank-you
for all your hard work.

Then she pats herself on the chest
and smiles.

How do you think
I got this fancy apron?

Giorgos (Gio)

I feel the sting of the handcuffs

as I stare through the gray fog
at the Statue of Liberty.

I am in the land of the free,
but I am in chains.

We wait and watch

the mass
of ticketed passengers
disembark.

The attendants sit at tables,
take names,
write them into ledgers,
sort people
into groups.

After the crowd clears,
an armed marshal
barks orders at us.

We line up.

They march us off the boat.

Directly
into a jail cell.

I lie to the guards

I tell them that I am an orphan.
I tell them I am seventeen.

They can't understand
what I'm saying.

They pull up
eyelids
with a buttonhook.

They examine:
mouths
nails
ears
teeth.

They pull a woman from the group,
mark her with chalk.

The letter H on her sleeve.

They take away one man
with pink eyes.

They sequester
a sallow-skinned girl,
who pinches
her cheeks
to make them appear
rosy, healthy.

The prisoners of Ellis Island

are Italian, Russian, Slavic,
Arabic, and German.

We do not speak to each other.
We do not want to be sent back. [22]

They slide porridge

under the bars
of the cell.

It's swimming
with mealworms.

One of the inmates gags
and slides it back.

I spend an hour
picking the
sleek, brown
bodies
out of the oats
so that I can eat.

I wake early in the morning

There is a man in a uniform
standing above me.

They tell me you want to be
a citizen of the United States
of America.

Is that right, boy?

I don't quite understand.

I hear the words
citizen of the United States
of America.

I nod yes.

Well, I have
a pretty good idea
how we can make
that happen
for you.

He leaves
a pressed and folded
U.S. Army uniform
at the foot of my bed.

They wait two weeks
and then load me onto
a ship.

This time with a ticket
to France.

Jeanne

I teach Vera

how to pry
small, black mussels

from the gray boulders
next to the salty sea.

Just like my father
taught me.

We search the sand
for tiny bubbles
rising from
the razor clams
buried deep
within the silt.

Vera looks out
at the green water.

I want to know
what she knows,
the world beyond
this harbor.

We fill our baskets
with black and gray jewels.

When they are full,
we strap them to our backs,
wade in the shallow water
and splash each other.

Mouths wide open
with laughter.

Our freckled faces
kissed by the sun.

At my mother's house

we rinse sand
from the shells.

Our maid, Anne,
helps us
mince garlic
and shallots.

We cook them in a large pot
with white wine
until the lovely smell
of cooking garlic
rises through the house,
seeps out of the windows
and onto the street.

The people
passing by
stop to close their eyes

and think about
all the beautiful meals
they have eaten
throughout their lives

and the friends
who have sat at their
tables

after a perfect day
at the beach.

Letter #12

November 1, 1918

When did you know that you loved me?
When you first heard my voice?
When you first saw my face?
When your lips touched mine?

Come back.

There are many more first things to experience.

Forever yours,
Petit Oiseau

On Sunday

we kiss things.

The icons
at the entrance
of the nave.

Theotokos,
the Mother of God.

We cross ourselves.

The thumb
and two fingertips
pressed together
for the Holy Trinity.

We kiss
the priest's hand.

We kiss
each other
before communion.

Christ is in our midst.

    He is and shall be.

We place the chalice
to our lips, and we drink.

Leave the church
walking backward,
bow and cross ourselves
again.

Grateful.
The service is done.

As usual

after the liturgy,

Dimitris
is waiting for me.

The women
swirl
as they fetch coffee
and biscuits
for their men.

That coffee smells good.

He motions to the table.
Empty handed.

I am expected
to serve him.

I walk up,
pour a cup
from a bronze urn.

I turn toward him,
hold my pinky up.

Take a slow sip,
not taking my eyes
from his.

You're right, Dimitris.
The coffee is good.

I walk away
to find my sister.

My shy sibling

is surrounded
by old women.

Her eyes say, *Save me.*

I pull her away
from the crowd.

Thank goodness.

Mrs. Manikas was talking
about her gout.

> *Let's leave before anyone*
> *starts talking*
> *about needlepoint.*

Or lower-back pain.

> *Or your*
> *future marriage*
> *to an eligible*
> *bachelor*
> *in the community.*

Let me grab my coat.

On the walk

I prepare myself.

We stop walking
in front of Sacred Heart.

Will you tell Mama
that I'm working
at the clothing drive tonight?

> *I thought*
> *we were walking home*
> *together.*

They need me.
I'll be back late.

Don't forget
to tell Mama where I am.

I open
the heavy side door
and slip inside
before
she can say
another word.

I lied to my sister.

I lied
to my best friend.

For a boy.

The last time I was here

I stashed my dress
in a paper sack

hidden
behind a heavy
potted plant
in the ladies' lavatory.

I sneak
through the dark corridors,
barely breathing.

The door creaks
as I open it.

It's still there.

I've always imagined

what it would be like
to act in a play.

To wear a costume
or a mask.

Assume
the personality
of another.

Feel the applause
from an audience
that adores you.

As I walk down
the street toward
the ferry dock,
I feel like everyone
in the world
is looking.

They see me.
Admire me.

This different version
of me.

I arrive early

circle the landing,
try to find Billy.

He's not here.

I close my eyes
and take a deep breath.

Mary.

I open my eyes.
He's standing in front of me.

Wearing a black suit,
white shirt,
and a black bow tie.

His eyes are wide.

He's holding
a white gardenia
in the palm
of his hand.

He tries to secure the flower

to my shoulder,

stabs himself with the pin
and winces in pain.

It's ok, I can do it,
I say and take the flower.

His hands are shaking.

I pin the corsage
above my heart and smile.

The smell
hits me,
wild
and sultry.

I take his hand.

We board the ferry boat
Sappho.

The sun sinks
lower,
creating a golden pathway
over the water

as the sky above us
turns pink
and orange.

La Belle Isle

feels like another world.

Across the river,
the skyline
in the distance.

My home
so close, so far.

Throngs of wealthy,
pink-cheeked
men and women,
dressed in their Sunday best,
stream off the ferry.

The weather has turned
and the first shades
of red
tip the leaves.

Partners
huddle together to stay warm.

I shiver.

I'm ashamed
to cover
my dress with my
well-worn
black
wool coat.

Billy puts his arm
around me and asks,

*Should we go
into the conservatory?* [23]

It's warmer in there.

We walk toward
a huge glass dome
and enter a steamy haven
of green.

The plants make me feel

like a stranger.

Wendy
in Neverland.

We walk though
a room filled with
palm trees.

I've only seen their shape
in books
and drawings
of faraway
desert islands.

Then a dry,
hot room with cacti
as tall as the roof
and blooming flowers
the size of my hand.

Underneath the glass dome
the showroom
holds flowers
of all shades of red,
open and bold.

Then the tropical house
filled with orchids
and ferns,
a statue of a little girl
pouring water
from a bowl.

Each room
more spectacular
than the last.

We are greedy.

Laugh
as we nudge
our noses into every flower,
gather
all the sweetness.

Before we enter

the dance pavilion,
I can hear
the orchestra playing.

We walk
from the darkness
into a brightly lit room,
stand underneath
a gigantic crystal chandelier.

The perimeter
of the hall
lined with tables
covered in white linen
and candles.

We settle at a table.

Billy orders us both
prime rib
and mashed potatoes.

The meat arrives
covered in juices,
so soft
it cuts with a fork.

I think of the meat
we eat at home,
boiled for hours.

The dessert arrives.

Berries dripping
over a crisp
whipped meringue
pavlova.

It disappears
in my mouth,
a heavenly cloud.

I pull Billy

onto the dance floor.

He holds me close
and puts his cheek
next to mine.

The lead singer moans
into the microphone.

Billy moves slowly
around the floor,
guiding us
through other couples
in their own trance.

I close my eyes and stop thinking.

Everything moves slowly,
sweet and viscous as honey.

My feet glide,
trusting
we will move together.

We sink deeper
into the velvet notes
of the music.

Eventually
the sound of the band
is replaced
by the piercing
staccato
of couples clapping.

Billy and I,
nose to nose.

Still breathing together
on the dance floor.

The wind is blowing

as we board the ferry.

My eyes
start weeping.

I want to tell him
about Dimitris,
my father's failing store.

The words are frozen.

The lies I have told.

I wish
I could make him understand
this can never be.

It starts to rain hard

We run
to the corner of the boat,
behind the stairwell
to hide.

He squeezes me
into his chest
with just the right
pressure.

He tips my head up
with two fingers.

He looks worried.
You're crying.

I can't stop
weeping.

He's so close.

Closer than anyone
has ever been.

Both hands on my face,
wiping my tears,
his entire body
covering mine.

Still moving around me,
dancing.

He touches
his forehead
to mine.

Mary, please.

He does not know
my yearning.

He does not know
there is no need
to beg.

On Sundays

we kiss things.

The golden chalice
of his lips.

When you finally have your first kiss

you may feel slightly dizzy.

You may feel
like you've been lifted
by a gust of wind.

You may feel
so full of air
that you can't breathe,
and you may
have to let it out
slowly
all the way home
like a balloon.

Squealing
as it floats
and flies.

You may feel
deflated.

When you realize
even balloons
have to come back
to earth
sometime.

Mary! Where have you been?

My mother
is standing in the doorway.

All of the lights are on.

Giorgos (Gio)

U.S. Army, Northwestern France
1917

How did I get here?

An accident.

Two boats
across the Atlantic,
a U.S. Army
uniform,
and now I am
in the middle of nowhere
with people
who don't speak
my language.

I miss
the teal green waters
of my homeland.

Why am I fighting
a war
that I don't
understand?

For a new beginning.
For possibility.
For freedom.

In my dreams,
the olive groves
call for me
to return.

We walk across France

in formation.

Our boots stomp
into the mud.

Our guns rest
on our shoulders.

The barrels point
toward the sky.

It feels like
we have been walking
for years.

My feet are blistered,
wet from the rain.

They smell
like rotten meat.

One of the soldiers in my company

helps me learn English
before we go to sleep.

His name is Pete.

He is kind and patient
but laughs
when I struggle
to make the sounds.

My mouth feels like
it is chewing
on a tough piece
of leather.

A soldier hands us blankets.

If the Germans don't get you,
the flu will.

I wrap myself in green wool
like a caterpillar
encircling itself
in a cocoon.

The cold night air
reaches its fingers
through
the fabric.

I miss my mother.

Out of town a little ways

I find a road lined with apple trees.
It leads to an abandoned house.

Bullet holes
scattered across
the side of the building.

The garden has turned.

The pumpkins
have spilled their seeds
and they are waiting
like soldiers at the front
finally called to duty.

The pigs are starving in their pen.

A porcelain tea set
is arranged on the garden table.

There is room for four.

A girl is walking
the rows
of fruit trees
with a bundle
in her arms.

It's a baby
wrapped in a blanket.

I am afraid
to ask
if the child
is alive.

In my imagination

Violetta holds her new baby
and walks home
through
the olive groves.

The early evening sun
casts a soft light
across the fields.

She wears a billowing shirt
and her pinstriped pants.

The baby is wrapped
in the white lambskin
Costas brought
to our house
so many
months ago.

My mother sets the table.

Roasted meat on their plates.
Baklava swimming
in honey.

They smile at the baby.

The war
has not touched them.

Jeanne

SAINT-MALO, FRANCE
1917

There's a stove

in the middle of the room
to keep the boys warm.

A wood pile
on the side of the building,
where I gather fuel.

Each time
I enter the building,
my arms overflow
with logs.

Back busted
from caring heavy loads.

Leaning over beds,
changing sheets,
and dressing wounds.

I check each boy for fever.
Adjust covers and pillows.

It's my job to make sure
everyone is comfortable
and clean.

To keep
the flames burning.

The more I check
the more I clean
the more I disinfect

the more likely it is
that a boy gets to keep
his leg.

We need blood!

A doctor stumbles
though the door.

I'm O positive.

He pulls on my arm
and takes me to surgery.

An unconscious boy
lying on the table.

I sit on a chair next to him.

Turn my eyes
away from his open
wounds.

A fellow nurse
smiles at me
while she pierces my vein.

Runs a tube
directly from me
to the patient.

I think about my father.

Imagine him
in a land far away.

Trying to help
one soldier
at a time.

My blood flows
from my arm
into the wounded boy.

I know
my father
would be proud.

Letter #13

November 2, 1918

My love,

I pray I can be the person you want me to be.

This fire, this anger, feels like it is consuming me.

I have done things for which I am ashamed.

How will the guilt and grief ever stop burning?

How can I be anything else?

How will I be able to go home?

I want to be yours forever,
Loup

My mother grabs my dress

holds
the green silk fabric
in her hand.

Her face
full of disappointment
and disbelief.

Marguerite went to Sacred Heart.

It was locked.

We know
you weren't there, Mary.

Your sister
walked in the storm
for hours
searching for you.

She's in bed with a fever.

Where were you?

  I was safe.

Where?

  I took the ferry to Belle Isle.

  To go dancing.

Enough!

My father holds his head
as if
I am splitting him
in two.

You will marry Dimitris
as soon as we work out
the details.

> *But Baba!*
> *I am almost done with school!*

> *I could graduate!*
> *And get a job!*

Nonsense!
A girl doesn't need
a job.

Especially
when her husband owns
a successful business.

It's over, Mary. Stop fighting!

Your sister is ill
because of you.

> *I met a boy, Baba.*
> *He cares for me.*

> *His family has money,*
> *and he's very sweet*
> *and kind.*

Who is this boy
who lives outside of our neighborhood?

Who doesn't understand our culture?

He takes you dancing
but makes no promises!

Doesn't he know
that lying
is not the best way to gain
a father's approval?

       Baba, I think you would like him.

I have already found you a man, Mary.

A man of substance.
A man who understands our family.

He has made a proposal.
I have accepted.

I will not go back on my word.

The next day

my father closes the store.

He looks at me
like a dog
that cannot be trained

as he places
a FOR SALE sign
in the window.

They say
God gives you only
what you can
handle.

Why
did God
give him me?

Marguerite's fever

is high,
and her throat hurts.

Mama gives
her warm honey water
and lets her stay home
from school.

I walk to school
with my brothers.

John shakes his head.

*I've never seen
Baba so angry.*

*You're making
the rest of us
look like angels.*

Gus swats John
in the stomach
and says,

*It'll get better.
They can't stay angry forever.*

Jim puts his hand
on my shoulder.

I don't feel comforted.

Will Marguerite
forgive me?

Giorgos (Gio)

A foxhole

sounds so calm.

A den carved into
a mound of dirt.
A safe space
for animal babies
to sleep.

This hole
that I am digging
for myself
feels like a grave.

At night, we sit in the trenches

and tell stories.

It helps with the waiting.

Some of the lucky ones
talk about their girlfriends.

They show letters
covered in red lipstick kisses
and perfume.

Pete has a girl, back in Detroit.

He tells me
her lips are soft
as a ripe nectarine.

I keep her letter right here,
close to my heart,
he says as he pats
his breast pocket.

Maybe you should keep it in your pants!
shouts one of the boys.

Laughter erupts
all around us.

I light a cigarette,
and then help Pete
light his.

We never light three cigarettes
in a row.

Not when it's dark.

One, they spot you.
Two, they sight you.
Three, they kill you.

Snow

We have entered
a fairyland.

The world is covered
in white.

The water is frozen
and so are our feet.

Frost,
with a hand in the air,
waves his wand
and invites the wind
to dance around
our sleeping bodies.

Everything is cold.

I can't fill my lungs
with air.

I dream that my father

is standing over my bed,
watching me sleep.

He has a worried expression
as if he has lost a lamb
in the hills
or there's a snake
next to his foot.

He reaches out his hand
to touch my shoulder.

*Giorgos, you need to wake up
now.*

My eyes snap open

I grab my rifle.

There are firebombs
bursting
all around me.

Faceless men are everywhere.
The horses are screaming.

I hear the moan
of fighter-bombers
overhead.

I don't know
in which direction to run.

There's not even a moon.

A corporal yells,
Shoot, for God's sake!
Shoot!

I plant my feet
and hold my gun tight
against my shoulder.

I fire as many bullets
as I can
into the men
running toward me.

I don't know
who I have shot.

I see a man writhing in the mud

He's holding his belly,
crying for help.

I rush to him
and struggle
to put his arm
around my body,
to pull him up
from the ground.

I can't see anything.

I wipe
the mud
from my eyes.

There's a letter tucked into his breast pocket.

I grab the gasmask
hanging on his chest
and place it over
his face.

You're going to be OK, Pete.
We're going to be OK.

The land smells like
gun smoke,
blood,
and urine.

I hear a crack
and a buzz.

We fall
to the ground.

Then nothing.

Jeanne

Nurses run down

the hallway
giggling,
rushing

to make it
to the impromptu
performance

of Shakespeare's
Midsummer Night's Dream
in the mess hall.

Someone
blows a toy horn.

Two sheets are drawn
to create a stage.

Vera and I

circle around each other

dressed like
the Fairy King Oberon
and his Queen Titania.

Flowing robes
and flower garlands
in our hair.

Unable to stop
laughing,
we recite our lines
from a shared script.

Our audience,
mildly amused patients,
slump in their chairs.

One boy drinks
loudly through a straw.

Milk dribbling
down his chin.

Another farts in his sleep.

Quiet!
a fellow soldier
elbows him awake.

The doctor
playing Lysander
consoles
his beloved Hermia,

The course of true love never did run smooth.

We hear a siren blaring

and glimpse the lights
of an ambulance
shining
in the courtyard.

Our jovial moment
broken.

The doctor
playing Lysander
sheds his costume
and sprints
toward the siren.

We gather the patients.

Is it over?
one boy mumbles
in his sleep.

I help him
back to his bed.

If only
I could convince him
the night,
his injuries,
the war
were all
just a dream.

Letter #14

November 3, 1918

This war feels like a virus.

No medicine can cure it—only patience—while we wait for the sickness to run its course.

I will do my best, as a nurse, to help heal the wounded and my country.

I pray that we will all be well soon.

Yours,
Petit Oiseau

When we get home from school

Marguerite's cheeks
are white
and she has a scarf
around her neck.

I try to cozy
next to her,
real close,
so I can whisper
into her ear.

But Mama
starts yelling,
Don't you go close to her!

I give her a kiss
on her cheek.

That night,
I get the fever too.

Everything is blurry

My mother
places a cold cloth on my forehead
and sings to me
in French.

Celui que mon coeur aime tant
Il est dessus la mer jolie
Petit oiseau tu peux lui dire
Petit oiseau tu lui diras
Que je suis sa fidèle amie
Et que vers lui je tends les bras. [24]

The air feels
as thick as
black tar.

I cannot move.

The one my heart loves so much
He is above the pretty sea
Little bird you can tell him
Little bird you will tell him
That I am his faithful friend
And that toward him I extend my arms.

My mouth is sticky
and words won't leave
the tip
of my tongue.

Marguerite is beside me
moaning,
saying my name.

I cannot even reach
for her hand.

I dream

that I'm dancing
under the crystal chandelier.

His hand presses
into my back.

His eyes say,
Come closer.

His cheeks say,
Soft. So softly.

His lips say,
Please.

My sister and I

are two sides
of a coin

molded
of the same
metal.

One head,
one tail

tossed
into the air.

We hold our breath.

Wishing,
praying.

The doctor marks a big, black X

on our front door.

Everyone in the house is quarantined.

Scarlet fever.

Our throats sore.
A bright-red rash
across our chests.

I stay in bed for a week,
sipping broth
and slowly get better.

Marguerite does not.

Giorgos (Gio)

U.S. Army, Northwestern France
1918

I wake in a field

ears ringing.

My fingers
shake up and down,
tapping
the moist earth.

I am alive.

My vision is blurry.

I can see shapes
coming in
and out.

I see a pile
of bloody soldiers.

My eyes focus
on a boy rifling
through pockets.

He finds
a pack of smokes
and some coins.

He sits
on the mound
of bodies.

Places coins
in his breast pocket
and lights
a smoke.

I hear gunshots
nearby.

They're killing
the wounded.

My eyes lose focus

my head slides back
to the earth.

Where is Pete?

A boot
kicks my leg.

I wince in pain.

Wait
for the gunshot
to my head.

A host of angels

lift me,
place me
in the hull
of a wooden boat.

I'm home again.

Bobbing
in the waves.

Silver fish glinting
underneath
the deep-blue water,
just waiting
to be caught.

A person hovers
over me.

Mouth opens,
mouth closes.

My eyes blur.

He pulls out
a roll of bandages,
circles them around
my head
until the world
is covered.

Where is Pete?

The armored truck
speeds along
a gravel path.

I feel the rhythm
of my sea
rocking me.

My boat.

I hear the bells
of heaven.

Ringing.

Jeanne

They tell me he's survived

a large blast
and he can't hear or see.

His head is bandaged.

I want this wounded boy
to know he's not alone.

I run my hand along the side
of the bedsheets
and then along his shoulder
and then down his hand.

He clamps onto my arm
and his body spasms
with intensity and fear.

He looks like he is running
from a wolf.

I call him

le loup, the wolf,

to remind him
of what
he has survived.

I tell him
we can be
*le loup et
le petit oiseau.*

*The wolf
and the little bird.*

Unlikely friends.

We can
work together.

To endure
even the harshest
winter.

The next day

I visit *le loup*
again.

I talk to him and tell him
someday
he will be well.

I tell him that his mother
loves him.

There are people
waiting for him.

He does not say a word,
but I hear his shallow breath,
and sometimes
he squeezes my hand.

His skin is darker than mine.

Even with a bandage
covering his face,
I can see
he is beautiful.

He is not willowy or thin
like most of the British
or French soldiers.

His chest is wide
and he has the large hands
and muscles
of a fisherman.

I feel embarrassed
when I look at him.

I fumble objects
and crash into carts.

He's the only soldier
that make my cheeks flush
and chest hurt.

He makes me check
my pulse.

I walk the hospital grounds

after work.

I stand on the rock wall
on my tiptoes
and look into
the dark-blue water
and the rocky shore.

Run my hand
along the stone tombs
in the graveyard
where *les corsaires*
are buried.

Privateers who stole
from foreign ships
and swore an oath
to give half
to their king.

I think about men
and their wars.

Alliances.

It makes me want to spit
on the ground.

Now
l'hospital du Rosais
is filled with soldiers
from many nations,
even Germans
who have been taken
as prisoners.

No matter which side
they are on,
they all believe
it is the right side.

Letter #15

November 4, 1918

My dearest,

I'm so sorry. This is all my fault. I thought we had more time.

Loup

After two weeks, I go back to school

Marguerite stays in our bed
wrapped in Mama's
thickest quilt.

Every day,
I come home
and tell her stories.

Some days,
she recognizes me,
and some days
she's in a dream.

I make a nest
of blankets and pillows
beside our mattress.

I can be near her at night,
but not disturb her.

It's cold on the ground.

I can hear the wind
howling through
the floorboards.

Gus hands me a note

I found this stuck
in the door.

Thought you might want it.

I open the envelope.

M–
When can we see each other again?
I can't stop thinking about you.
–B

How can I tell Billy
about the pain
we have caused?

The guilt I feel.

I fold the note,
hold it over the candle
on the table.

Open a window
and toss the letter out.

Watch
the burning bundle
fall
into the snow.

The temperature drops

My brothers and I
collect dry sticks and wood
on our walk home
from school.

As soon as we enter,
my mother makes
a roaring fire in the stove.

We all gather
around it

thaw our frozen fingers
still stinging
from the wind.

The X has worn off.

Marguerite is still sick.

The doctor says
her fever
has become rheumatic.

My mother fills
a hot water bottle.

I bring it up to our room.

Marguerite's thin,
but she's sitting up,
supported
by pillows.

I pray this dreadful
illness will go away.

I want my sister back.

I tuck the water bottle
under her legs
so she can't feel the bite
of the cold.

The doctor is here

for Mama,

heavy
with her sixth child.

He looks at me.

*She cannot
get sick
with the fever.*

It's bad for the baby.

*She must do less
around the house.*

By this
he means
all the women's work

that he would never
ask my brothers
or my father
to do.

My father puts two cots

in the cellar

for wandering folks
who have lost their jobs
and need a place to stay.

He says we must
help people in need.

Mama hates it.

I have children here!
These are rough men.

Baba insists.

White men.
Black men.

All are welcome.

Even though
we don't have very much,
we still have more than
some.

The men join us for dinner

I listen to them talk to each other
as I make a big pot of broth
with the remaining
onions
and carrots
and potatoes
from our fall garden.

They are angry
and shouting.

There's no unemployment insurance,
no national relief
for the poor!

Half the people
in Detroit
are unemployed!

Henry Ford's
still making
thirty million dollars
a year!

One of the wanderers is named James

He nods his head
while the other men are talking
and says,

My father was a slave.
He was freed as a boy.

I grew up thinking
my country was offering me freedom.

A chance to work and learn.

Now I hear you, there's no good jobs.

There's even less for Black men.

James takes a sip of his soup
and continues,

They won't even let us rent or buy houses
in good neighborhoods. [25]

They put on the lease:

No negroes.

No foreign born.

No undesirables.

He tells us
they're planning to build a wall
on Pembroke Avenue.

To separate
the Black and brown neighborhoods
from the white ones. [26]

Foreign born

Why did my parents come to America?

It feels
like we have nothing.

No land.
No family.

We are drifting
in a world of strangers
who are as lost
as we are.

After dinner

one of the wanderers pulls
a violin from his sack.

Puts the instrument
to his chin
and jerks his bow
over the strings
in the hopping rhythm
of a jig.

For the first time
in months,
people are smiling
at the table.

Baba even carries Marguerite
downstairs
and holds her on his lap,
swaying to the music.

The fiddler
stands in the middle
of our kitchen.

Pounding his foot
into the floor.

Marguerite lifts herself to her feet
and begins to dance.

We all gasp.

Baba jumps up
to join her.

He twists and twirls her
to the music.

James asks Mama
to dance.
My brothers and I
join too.

I close my eyes

and feel the rhythm
of the music
enter my heart.

Hope.

In the middle of the night

I hear Marguerite
talking in her sleep beside me.

I jostle her,
but she won't wake up.

I feel her forehead.

She's burning.

I run to tell Mama
to call for the doctor.

He examines Marguerite.

The fever
is affecting her
lungs and heart.

In the morning

I lie next to Marguerite
and tell her
a story

about two sisters
who love
each other
so much
they build a sailboat
out of their
aprons

and use
their mother's broom
to paddle through
the air.

Marguerite opens
her eyes
and then closes
them again.

How will it end?
she asks,
her voice as meek
as a church mouse.

I grab her hand
and squeeze it.

I'll tell you when I get home.

All day I think about

how the story will end.

When I return home,
she and my mother
are gone.

I ask our neighbor, Mrs. O'Malley.

They couldn't wait, love.
They had to go.

The hospital.

No one
in our family
has ever been
to the hospital.

I start to cry.

My father and brothers and I

stay up all night.

We sit at the kitchen table
and say nothing.

In the early morning light,
my mother comes home.

She's alone.

She drops to her knees.

My father runs to her.

She is not weeping.

She looks at him
with eyes like stones
that have been dropped
into cold, dark water

and says,

I couldn't save her.

I run out the door

down the street

keep running

lungs heaving
for breath.

I run until I reach
the apple orchard

filled with the
gray bones
of winter trees.

I scream.

Until all the air
has left my body
and my lungs
begin to rattle and moan.

I fall into the snow
and stay there.

My body shakes
on the frozen ground.

The sky is
filled with gray
storm clouds
that look like they will burst
at any moment.

I can't stand up.

A branch breaks
next to me.

An arm's distance away
stands a fox.

Her shining red coat
bright against the white
of the snow.

She looks at me.

Her amber eyes
hold me

until she darts

into the rows
and rows
of trees.

I am alone.

I am alone.

Giorgos (Gio)

U.S. ARMY, NORTHWESTERN FRANCE
1918

Through the ringing

I hear a woman
whispering to me.

Her voice sounds
like a forest
alive with green vines
and flowers.

She smells
of perfumed earth.

The weight
of her hand,
a river stone
rolled smooth.

She places her cheek
on my palm.

Sing me to sleep.
Sing me home.

Everything hurts

Lift my hands.

Squeeze my hands.

Lift my arms.

Run my hands
over my belly
and chest.

Check for holes.

Rotate my foot.

Feel the bandages
covering my eyes.

All of my fear

swims
under my eyelids

trapped

a blanket
of darkness.

I can't breathe.

Doctor.
Doctor.
Doctor.

I pray
for color, light.

Please, God,
don't take my sight.

Jeanne

SAINT-MALO, FRANCE
1918

I walk the ramparts

on my way to work.

The ball of the sun
at the edge of the water.

An egg yolk
breaking
over the white plate
of the sky.

The hospital

is unusually quiet.

Vera and I exchange
une bise sur la joue,
a kiss on each cheek
in greeting.

She tells me
about her dinner.

The first time eating
loup de mer—sea bass—
au beurre blanc.

I could bathe in that sauce!
she squeals.

I try to keep a straight face
as Vera acts
like a fat man
stuffing her face
with fish,
wiping greasy sauce
from her chin
with her apron.

Madame Leroux
glares at us
and hands me clipboards
with charts
to update.

Vera whispers,
Out of all the fish in the sea,
the loup
is clearly the best!

Then gives me
a knowing wink
and blows me a kiss.

From across the room

I hear *mon loup*
crying out for help.

I run to grab the surgeon.

Several of the trained nurses
come as well.

They close
the circle of curtains
around him.

When they finally
pull the drapes,
his bandages are off.

I've wondered
many times
about the shape
of his face.

The color of his hair.

I can't bring myself to look.

For hours,
I visit each bed
except his.

What am I afraid of?

Letter #16

November 10, 1918

How can we risk love—when it can be lost?

It is the most fragile task.

Hold this bubble in your hand. Look at the rainbow globe and how it swirls.

Imagine a perfect world inside.

Then ask yourself, how long will it last?

Yours,
Petit Oiseau

Before my first breath

before my mother held me
and called me
by my name.

Before my body unfurled
like a fern growing
into the light.

Before I spoke
my first word.

Before this, I knew
I was not alone.

There was another body.

Another heart beating
next to mine.

My sister is in a wooden box

I speak to her in a whisper.

There were once
two sisters

who loved each other
so much
they built a sailboat
out of their
aprons

and used
their mother's broom
to paddle through
the air.

They traveled
way up
into the heavens

so they could live
in the clouds

and eat cake
and chocolate pudding.

Sometimes,
they hurt each other,

but they forgave
everything

because they were sisters.

*Always together
in the golden light
of the sun.*

Elena holds my hand

for an hour.

She tries to comfort me.
She feels the pain too.

I can't talk.
I sit and stare.

The light leaves the room.
The guests return home.

Until it is only me.

On the sofa,
staring at the window
wondering

how things
could have possibly
gone so wrong.

I hear my mother weeping in the kitchen

Other than giving birth,
I have never heard my mother cry.

She's sitting over a wash bin
filled
with the soiled clothing
of her children.

She's using her treasured
silver
serving spoons
to do the laundry
so her hands
won't touch
the poisonous,
flesh-eating lye.

Chemicals
to get the sick
out of the house.

I sit in a chair
and wrap my arms around her.

I know she wishes
she could raise her children
in a beautiful house on the ocean
with clean white linens
and crystal vases filled
with lavender.

But all she has left
is a cold house
and a husband without a job.

Her daughter has died.

And the years
of hard work, poverty, and illness
have eroded
the polished silver life
of her youth
into the red, cracked hands
of grief.

My mother is a beautiful person

She is beautiful
when she helps people
in the neighborhood.

She is beautiful
when she makes her children laugh.

She is beautiful
when she stands at the sink
and the light shines
on her hair and she is lost
in her thoughts.

My mother
is also a beautiful writer.

And so she decides
to write to
Eleanor Roosevelt.

She tells her how she loves
this country
even though there are no jobs
and Christmas is coming.

She tells her
she cannot feed her children
and she is watching
their cheeks hollow.

She tells her
she has already lost one child

and she cannot
and will not
lose another.

My teacher pulls me aside

after school.

Mary, I can't even imagine
how much you must miss
your sister.

I want
to say to her,
I feel like I live
in a glass case.

Sleeping Beauty.

When I see the animals
pressing their faces
to the glass,
I just lie there.

Do nothing.
Say nothing.

While the world
moves around me.

I dream

of children
bobbing up and down
on pink and white
painted ponies.

The carousel spins.

A monkey
in a scarlet vest
dances
as a man
turns the handle
on an ornate music box.

The sound distorted.

Speeding up
and slowing down.

A needle
being adjusted
on the surface of a record.

I see my sister spinning
on the wheel.

No beginning and no end.

She reaches
to capture
a golden ring
from a lion's mouth.

The scene turns dark gray.

My sister
becomes a shadow.

I see Billy
standing at the gate.

His cheeks shine
pink,
ruby lips,
eyes the color
of robin eggs.

He's smiling at me,
holding out his hand.

A beacon of color
in a black-and-white world.

Giorgos (Gio)

U.S. ARMY, NORTHWESTERN FRANCE
1918

Without my bandages

I can see everything.

Boys crying,
asking for help.

Wrapped severed limb
leaking blood
onto the mattress.

A soldier wanders
between the beds,
speaking to his sister
who's not
in the room.

I close my eyes.

Cover my ears
with a pillow.

Where is the woman
who smells like flowers
and forest?

Jeanne

SAINT-MALO, FRANCE
1918

I tell myself

to go to him.

His eyes are closed,
but I sit next to him
and hold his hand

just like usual.

He opens his eyes
and they are black
as storm clouds.

His face looks damaged
and beautiful

a tree struck by lightning.

It's you,
he says softly and looks at me
with a fearful expression.

Are you well? What do you need?

I feel his head
to make sure
there is no fever.

*I didn't know
you were so beautiful,*
he says.

I blush as red as a cardinal

He speaks English slowly
with an accent
just like I do.

I wonder where he's from,
but instead I ask,

Do you have a name?

He closes his eyes
and for a moment
I think he has fallen asleep.

Then he takes
a deep breath
and says,

My name is Giorgos,
but my friends call me

Gio.

Gio's face is weary

He needs sunshine.

I wrap a wool blanket
around his legs
and wheel him
through the grounds
of the hospital.

We rest
beside a small pond
which provides
some comfort.

He tells me about
his sister and mother.

I miss the smell of the dry hills.
The warmth of the sun.

I imagine his home.
His land.

The view
of a completely different sea.

He stops talking
when a fleet
of fighter-bombers
buzzes overhead
so low
it feels like they
are coming for us.

Gio jerks and shields
his head with his arms
and shrieks
with the pain of someone
who has been hit.

The fear
of the Western Front
still alive
in his muscles.

I think about the plane

my father took me to see
so long ago.

The beautiful,
fragile
invention

built to give
mortal men
the power of the gods

has now become
a machine of war.

He shudders

with cold and fear.

Reaches
for the blanket
but can't manage
to grab the corner.

I fold it over his shoulders
and tuck it
into the corners
of the wheelchair.

I want to make him warm
and calm.

I've always wanted
to have an adventure.

To leave
these granite walls.

I'm envious
of what you've seen.

He looks at the pond.
Eyes black, round stones.

He does not look at me
when he says,

I'm glad
that you have not seen
what I have seen.

He tells me

he will begin a new life
after the war.

In the United States
of America.

A country
with so much land
they give it away.

A country
filled with large cities,
factories,
and smokestacks

and jobs
for strong, willing
men.

DETROIT, MICHIGAN
1933

Letter #17

November 6, 1918

My dearest love,

When I think I cannot endure another moment of this awful war, I think about our future children.

Well-fed and strong.

As many as possible.

I think they will be our greatest joy when we need it most.

Always and forever yours,
Loup

My boots

are made of concrete.

My lungs can't hold breath.

I'm scared
I'm not going
to reach her in time.

I knock
loud and hard
so she can hear me.

The midwife answers the door
with disheveled hair
and sleep in her eyes.

The baby is coming!

We run through the alleyway
and climb the stairs
to our apartment.

My mother is lying in her bed
screaming.

My brothers and father
are gathered
at the door
with scared looks
on their faces.

I pray to every god
I can imagine,
to anyone who might
hear me,

Please don't let my mother die.

The midwife

makes my brothers
leave the room
but lets me stay.

I hold my mother's hand
as she tries
to squeeze her pain
into my body.

I put my face close to hers.

I don't want her
to suffer alone.

My mother screams
like a banshee
and then she is silent.

Just when I think
she won't ever
take another breath—

I hear a baby cry.

My mother is a flower

that has been drenched by a storm.

All the women
climb onto the bed,

a lifeboat floating
on a turbulent sea.

All eyes are
on the small creature
lying on my mother's chest.

He suckles at her breast,
surveying
his brand-new
world.

Eleven Greek superstitions for a new baby

1

Give a spoonful of honey to the baby
when you visit the house for the first time.

The baby will have a sweet life.

2

Never wash the baby's clothing at night.
Bad spirits or the devil will come.

Wash them during the day and hang them in the sun.

3

Don't let the baby look in the mirror
or his soul will slip away.

4

A new mother must not be seen
in public for forty days.

This is because people are jealous of her.

5

Babies are named after their grandparents.

6

The godparents should buy the baby
the first pair of shoes.

7

The baby's hair should not be cut
before the baptism.

8

If you put money under the baby's pillow,
he will have a prosperous life.

9
Spit to avoid the evil eye.

For example:
Your baby has beautiful cheeks.

Ptu, Ptu, Ptu.

10
Put a gold pin with a blue eye
on the baby to keep him safe.

11
If you do all of these things,
your baby
will be blessed. [27]

This baby is called Pierre

But I call him *my* baby.

I am the one
who holds him.

I am the one
who changes him.

I am the one
who comes
when he cries.

I am not old enough
to have a child
of my own.

I will practice
with Pierre.

He is almost
mine.

I wish Marguerite could hold him

In my mind,

I tell her about his tiny toes
and his little smile.

She would love to see him grow.

He is beginning
to hold his head up
by himself.

His cheeks are fat
with milk.

My father wanted to give Pierre

a Greek name.

My mother said,
We speak your language,
we eat your food,
we live in a country
of your choosing,

but I am FRENCH.

This baby
is going to have a
FRENCH name.

When my father protested,
she slammed her broom
to the floor.

You've named all the boys.

Augustus after your father.
John after Yiannis, your priest!

I want to honor my family.

It is my turn to name a son.

She named Pierre
after her father,
who was a doctor.

I wonder
if he would like to know
that our new baby
has his name.

I wonder
if he would have known
how to make Marguerite
well again.

Uncle Pete and Aunt Irma

arrive
on Christmas Eve
carrying dishes
filled with hot food
bottles of wine
loaves of bread.

Hugs and kisses for all of us.

It is the role of the youngest daughter
to greet guests at the door
with a glass
and offer them a drink
and say the blessing
of the household:

May our relationship
be as sweet as honey,
as strong as salt,
as clear as water.

Marguerite and I used to argue
about who would greet
the guests.

Now, I am the only daughter.

The one to say the blessing
as the people in our lives
come and go.

When Greeks have known a friend

for a very long time, we say:

We have eaten bread and salt together.

That is how my father feels
about Uncle Pete.

He also fought
in the war.

When Uncle Pete leaves,
he puts his forehead
to my father's forehead

his hands
around his cheeks
like a brother.

They are not twins,
but they look
like they know

what the other one is thinking
without words.

After his friend has left

my father puts his arm
around me.

His voice softens.

Many things have happened
over the course of my life.

Sometimes I feel
like I have lost all of my eggs
and also the basket.

I am thankful
for all that we still have.

He hugs me
for the first time
since I was
a young child.

I am so angry with him.
I want to scream.

Why can't he accept
the life I want.

The man I want.

I can't.
I am too tired.

All I can do
is lean in and receive
his love.

I imagine Billy and his parents

in my home.

The vast chasm
between our two worlds.

In my mind,
my mother
serves spanakopita
and olives.

Billy's mother asks
if there is any meat
and potatoes.

My father offers her ouzo
and she holds
her palm up.

She belongs
to the temperance movement,
fighting to keep
prohibition alive.

His father is an engineer.

My father
never went
to high school.

Billy's mother is a
Daughter of the American Revolution.

I am the daughter of immigrants.

How can I
build a bridge to join
our two families?

Ask them to travel
such a distance?

At night

I quiet all the static.

I tune my brain,
my radio,
toward my sister's
frequency.

Can you hear me?

Who

will melt this crust of ice
in my veins?

Start my pulse.
Help me to breathe.

Who
will plant a bulb in the frozen earth?

Push and pulse
under
the snow.

Who
will puncture the land?

Where it seems
nothing
will ever
grow.

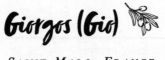

Early in the morning

I open my eyes.

Clear the sleep
from my vision.

Focus and blur.

I watch Jeanne
without her noticing.

She walks
around the room,
attending
to all the patients.

She comes to my bedside.

I pretend I am asleep.

She stays with me.
Feels my forehead,
strokes my hair.

Gently nudges me awake.

I open my eyes
and focus.

She's looking at me
with kindness
and concern.

Her cheeks pink with heat.

Each evening, I feel

my body improving.

Each morning,
I wake
with new pain.

It feels
like I am running a race
with a chair
tied to my leg.

Moving farther
down the road,
slower
than I want.

My body's entire weight

rests on the cane.

I move one leg,
then the other.

Every muscle in my body
searing in pain.

Jeanne supports me
as I slowly hobble
around the room.

The patients cheer.

Up and at 'em, soldier!

Atta, boy, Gio!

You got this, brother!

I try to write a letter

to my mother and Violetta.

I write a sentence
and then scratch it out.

I finally decide on
one line:

I am alive.

Jeanne

In the hospital

time is slow and sticky.

Each day
filled with broken
bodies.

Bodies that weep,
and ooze,
and shake.

Bodies that heal
and are sent back
to the front.

Bodies that are buried
in the graveyard
behind the chapel.

Some of the bodies
don't even
have a name.

Those are the most difficult.

Their mothers
don't know
where they are.

I spend time

with each patient.

I try to give them
the care they deserve,
but I always find my way back
to Gio.

No matter
how hard I try
to turn away.

I am
a compass needle
spinning north.

Gio's arm linked

to mine.

We take a short walk
around the courtyard.

He closes his eyes

and sucks
the fresh air
greedily
into his nostrils.

His chest fills
like a hot air balloon

and it seems
as though his feet

might lift off
the ground.

We sit by the pond

and take turns reading from
a book of John Donne poems.

Learning
English together,
giggling
at our mistakes.

Gio takes the book.

He reads well
for someone just learning.

His voice smooth
and his face is calm.

I close my eyes and listen
silently to the words,
until he reaches a poem
entitled
"To His Mistress
Going to Bed"
and begins to blush
and hesitate.

I snatch the book away
and tuck it under my apron.

I can't look at his face.

We fall into laughter.

Maybe not that one!

Every moment of each day

staring out of my window

lying in my bed

combing my hair

putting on my uniform

tending to my mother's garden

walking on the beach
before work begins

no matter what
I am doing

I am thinking about him.

I take Gio to the cemetery

and tell him
this hospital was built
by the King of France

for *les corsaires*
of Saint-Malo,
who stole ships and jewels
for the crown.

I've always been afraid
of privateers and pirates,
I say, shy to admit
my childhood fears.

He sits on a bench
next to a grave
and hangs his head.

If you are afraid of thieves,
you should be afraid of me.

I hold his hand
wait for an explanation.

I killed a man.

Letter #18

November 7, 1918

I get so frustrated—thinking I can do nothing.

Sitting here.

Staring out a window, while others fight for personal freedom and human decency.

What can I do?

I am a young woman—without money, without power.

I must do something.

Start small.

Study. Write. Believe in change.

Yours,
Petit Oiseau

On Christmas morning

there is a dusting of snow
on the ground.

We wake
to the early morning light,
pull our woolen
blankets closer
around our shoulders.

Mama starts the fire
in the woodstove
and puts on a kettle.

There is a knock.
We hear the door open.

Mama begins to laugh
and then cry.

We rush down the steps
and out of the apartment.

There is a long black
limousine
in front of the building,
with a Christmas tree
strapped to the top.

Two men in black suits
and top hats
with red poinsettias pinned
to their lapels
are singing
"In the Bleak Midwinter"

while unloading
wrapped gifts
and food
from the car.

All of the kids get presents

My brothers get spinning tops
and toy soldiers
and a popgun.

And I get
a white rabbit fur hat
that covers all of my curls
and matching mittens.

Marguerite
would have loved
the warmth
and softness.

My mother and father
get a turkey with stuffing
and a Christmas pudding
and decorations
and candles for the tree.

And my mother receives a card:

Dear Jeanne,

I read your letter.
I hope these humble gifts
help to bring joy
to your family.

Please have your husband report
to the Department of Human Resources
at the Ford Motor Company on Monday morning.
I have secured employment
for him there.

From our family to yours,
Merry Christmas,

Eleanor Roosevelt

I stand outside

watching the snow fall.

My new hat
makes me feel
like a Russian czarina
traveling across the tundra
in a horse-drawn sleigh.

Just as
I am about
to go in
I hear
a familiar rumble.

I close my eyes once
and open them.

A flood of emotion
enters me
as I see
a blond boy
driving
a Ford Cabriolet.

Where have you been?

I can't answer.

I can't stop kissing him
on his lips
on his eyelids.

He places his hands on my cheeks.

I was worried, Mary.

Really worried
that I had done something
wrong.

I know
eventually
I will have to tell him
about my lies.

My grief.

I press him
against the building
until he gives in.

Wraps his arms around me
until I can't breathe.

Until I can't feel
any more pain.

Will you marry me?

he asks,
holding my hand.

> *Billy, you know I can't.*

Because of your parents?

> *Yes, but also*
> *because we're so young.*

> *And I want more.*

Another man?

> *No.*
> *I want to be more*
> *than just a wife.*

You can have it all.
A job, a husband, children.

I can give you
everything
you want.

> *I just need some time*
> *to figure out*
> *what I want.*

I'm not going anywhere.
I can wait, Mary.

> *Can you?*

For a thousand years.

As long
as we keep kissing.

She drops my hands

and backs away
from me.

You're scaring me, Gio.

Jeanne, listen to me.

*My sister was pregnant
and starving.*

*I convinced my brother-in-law
to steal a lamb
for her.*

*He didn't want to.
He argued with me.*

*I told him
if he didn't want to help me,
I would do it myself.*

Finally, he came with me.

My voice catches,
and I wait.

*We both went to the mountains,
but only I returned.*

I didn't pull the trigger,
but I killed him, Jeanne.

I am crying now.

He would still be there
with my sister, with his child.

If it weren't for me.

She looks out at the sea

and doesn't say anything.

I can't stop telling her
how I feel.

I can't go home.
Not for a long, long time.
If I go back,
they'll send me to jail.

I pause
and reach for her hand.

I used to want to be a fisherman,
like my father.

Now, all I want is a family.

I want a wife.
I want children.

To be the father I never had.

To be the father
my sister's son never had,
because of me.

Her gray eyes are reflective pools.

There's a deep ache
in my chest.

I take a step closer
and she doesn't move
away.

Gio.

In one swift motion
I pull her to me.

Press
her body
and her lips
to mine.

She gasps

muscles taut,
aware
of the newness
between us.

She stays close,
her nose touching mine.

I can feel her
soft, short breaths.

Then
she looks at me
with wild eyes
and pulls away.

Runs
out of the cemetery
toward the hospital.

The gate swinging
behind her.

In my mind

I kiss her hand
when she feels my forehead.

I kiss her neck
when she bends over my bed.

I kiss her lips
in the hallway
when no one is looking.

I kiss her memory
when she has gone home.

I kiss her
all night long.

The doctor shakes me awake

Listens to my heart.
Takes my blood pressure.

Has me follow
a white light with my eyes.

Asks me to walk
around the room.

You're healing well, soldier.

He scribbles
some notes in my file.

I want to feel proud
of my recovery.

Instead,
I feel a sinking dread.

Jeanne

The Red Cross girls

and the volunteer nurses
decide to host a dance.

We decorate the hall with flags
and banners

and the girls
wax the floor four times
so it's as
slick as a ribbon. [28]

Soldiers come
from all the bases
nearby.

They arrive
packed into their trucks,
sitting on each other's laps.

They are singing love songs,
swigging from their canteens.

Cigarettes tucked
behind their ears.

Arms are wrapped
around each other's shoulders
like brothers.

Every soldier in Saint-Malo

except Gio.

Who shook his head
and pointed
to his cane.

The kiss
hangs between us.

A piece of fruit
swinging
slightly too far away
to grasp.

It is a moon dance

and there's a big, round moon
made of tin
with a painted face.

All the lights are turned out
except one pointed
at the big moon.

Six boys sit up in the balcony
with colored lamps

red, green, blue, and white. [28]

The boys turn
the colored lights on the floor

and the drums start beating
and arms start waving

and pretty soon the men
are throwing the women
into the air

legs hopping

like popcorn
in a hot oiled pan.

There are about four soldiers
for every girl,

so I dance the fox-trot,
the one-step, and the waltz
about one hundred times.

Some of the boys
are handsome.

Some of the boys are meek.

They all smell different.

I feel different
in each of their arms.

Vera and I take a break

Wave our hands
and shoo the boys away
like flies on a pie.

Vera scans the room
for handsome men.

She wants
to try all of them
before she chooses
one.

Vera dances
with a handsome captain.

I sit and watch
and think of Gio.

I wish
I could kiss him
again.

Tell him
what happened
wasn't his fault.

The music swells
and I close my eyes.

Imagine him swaying
to the music.

His cheek next to mine.

Repairing the damage
between us.

On the walk home

Vera thrums me
with questions
about which soldier
I like best.

She is smitten
with the American
she danced with several times.

He's tall,
wears his uniform well,
and smells
like a bar of fancy soap.

He is one tall, cool glass of water,
Vera says with a wink.

I sigh
and tell her
the boy I wanted
to dance with the most
wasn't there.

After we part

I stop under a streetlamp.

Lean my warm body
against a cool stone wall.

For a moment,
I think about sneaking
into the hospital.

I imagine lying down
next to him
in the same bed.

Kissing him
soft and slow.

I could be with him,
if I dared.

When I return home

Maman is crying.

A telegram
written on yellow paper
has fallen to the floor.

I pick it up
and read it.

Chère Madame,

*It is my painful duty to inform you
that a report has this day
been received
from the War Office
notifying the death of:*

*(N°) 16929
(Name) Pierre Prigent
(Regiment) 156th Foreign
(Date) 2 March, 1918
(Cause of Death) Tuberculosis*

*If any articles of private property
are found,
an application can be submitted
for their receipt.*

*I am,
forever,
your faithful servant,*

*S.R. Lauren
Officer in Charge of Records*

I stand up

without saying a word.

I walk out the door
into the night.

Tears streaming
down my face.

My body numb.
My mind buzzing.

I see a group of young people
huddled together,
returning home
from the dance.

They are clutching bottles,
swaying and laughing
as they navigate
the uneven cobblestones.

I walk to the rampart
and climb the stairs.

Stand on the edge
of the granite wall.

For a moment, I imagine
what would happen
if my body
fell to the rocks
below.

The ocean seems endless.

I lie down on my side
and wrap my arms
around my legs.

A windless sail
collapsing
into itself.

When I wake

the horizon is filled
with a dark, hazy light,
which becomes
an orange glow.

A red orb rises
clear and brilliant
out of the daze.

For a moment,
my body is covered
in light.

I rise and walk a gravel path
lined with giant
magnolia trees.

The branches thick
with black starlings.

I stand still and watch them.

Hundreds of birds
shriek and cackle
a murmuration
of deafening chatter.

Then with the suddenness
of raucous applause
erupting
at the end

of a grand performance

tous les oiseaux
take flight.

Maman won't get out of bed

I stay home with her
for several weeks.

I think of Giorgos,
but I don't want
to leave Maman.

I sit by her bedside.

Try to feed her
spoonfuls of soup,
small pieces of bread,
like she is one
of my patients.

She refuses
nourishment.

It feels like she is trying
to die.

Maman is burning

and she's talking
in a language that no one
can recognize.

The doctor arrives.

He touches
Maman's forehead
and applies his stethoscope
to her chest.

There is not much
we can do
except wait.

I wish my father were here.

I call for my aunt,
Sister Marie-Thérèse.

She arrives wearing
her traditional habit:
black tunic
white wimple
and black veil.

She hugs me fiercely.

Drops down on her knees
next to my mother's bed.

Now, she is in God's hands.

My aunt and I

pray together.

She holds the cross
around her neck
and presses it
to her forehead.

She prays to her Lord,
her Husband, and her Keeper.

I pray to my father.

Papa,

*if she walks
down the tunnel
toward that loving light,*

*tell God
and Saint Peter
waiting at the gate*

to put his golden keys away.

*Tell them to please
send her back to me.*

My God

doesn't listen.

The coroner comes.
He places a black blanket
over my mother's body
and lifts her
onto a stretcher.

They take her
through the front door
and load her
onto a wagon
pulled by six
black horses.

My God
turns the sky gray
and opens up the clouds.

My God
rains down
on me
with the thunder
of sorrow.

My God
has made me
an orphan.

Letter #19

November 8, 1918

My Petit Oiseau,

If I had all the money in the world, I would buy you a house and fill our gardens with roses.

I would feed you almonds and olives, and we could sit on the porch and stare at the clouds.

We could walk around our town—any town we chose as our home.

I would be proud to be your husband. Proud to call you my wife.

Your loving and loyal,
Loup

There's a Ford in your future

On the first day of his new job,
my father gathers
with all the new employees.

The workers fill
the factory floor.

They wait
for the initiation ceremony
to begin.

It is simple.

The employees
wear
their native costumes
from all around
the globe.

Embroidered vests from Poland.
Kaftan coats from Russia.
Sarape ponchos from Mexico.

My father wears
his fustanella—a traditional kilt,
a white billowy blouse,
and black vest
from Greece.

They walk together
into a huge
melting pot
large enough to fit
ten men.

When the cauldron tips,
all of the men
walk out

wearing the same
Ford factory
uniform.

Americans. [29, 30, 31]

Mama wants us to be presentable

She twists and ties
my hair
with strips
of cloth.

All night,
I struggle
to climb
the hills and valleys
poised
on the top
of my head.

I wake
in the morning
angry.

My head hurts
but it's full
of bouncing
curls.

I avoid the mirror.

Remember
the story of Medusa?

She was transformed
into a monster
because of her vanity.

We tour the foundry

It's red.
It's hot.
It's dangerous.

The floors are covered in sand.

White eyes
peek through
layers
of black soot.

I walk the line.

The noise
coming from
the machines
sounds
like music
rising up
from the depths
of hell.

Each day

my father stokes the flames
on the factory floor.

Shovels pig iron scrap,
hammers and drills.

Pours viscous
white heat
into the cauldrons.

When he comes home,
he smells
of sulfur and coke.

We hold our noses and shriek
as my mother pushes him

toward the backyard shower,
where he washes away

the dirt and grime
of a hard day's work.

He puts on a clean shirt.

We sit down to a simple meal
of bread and butter
and tomatoes.

He places both hands over his eyes
and says to all of us,

Thank God I have a job.

On Saturday

my father puts on a suit
and his best hat
and walks out of the door.

My mother follows after him.
Where are you going?

He looks over his shoulder and says,
Mind your own business, woman!

My mother sulks all day.

She worries that he's sick
or, worse,
he has found
a younger woman.

The truth is

even though

Modern.
American.
Women.

choose their husbands,
they still
have to serve them.

And they are tied
to their houses

like an eagle
held by its master's tether.

We hear frantic honking

in front of our building.

When we go outside
we see my father
with his hat tipped
up like a schoolboy.

He is smiling
from ear
to ear.

Standing in front
of a brand-new,
shining black
automobile.

He drives us around all day
in our new car.

It feels like we're traveling
on the back
of a giant
black dragon.

Shooting fire
and flying above
the long, gray roads
that lead straight
out of town.

It takes my brothers a week

before they learn to drive.

Gus takes his friends
to see a moving-picture show
at the theatre
on a Friday night.

John chauffeurs my father
to and from work.

I don't even ask.

Good Greek Girls
don't drive cars.

One night, my brother John

comes home drunk.

He's swaying
and can't get up the stairs
by himself.

Don't tell Mom and Dad!
he hisses.

I bring him his nightclothes
and assure him
I won't tell anyone
his secret.

If he teaches me
how to drive.

The next day

I get behind the wheel.

The black leather
feels soft and smooth
under my palms.

The road opens up.
I can see the whole world
in the windshield.

I am finally in control.

And I realize
nobody is ever
going to tell me to stay
in one place
again.

Giorgos (Gio)

SAINT-MALO, FRANCE
1918

My stomach

is in knots.

I should have gone to the dance.

Will she
think of me
while she's out
in the world
having fun?

I pray
she doesn't meet
another person.

A better person.

Will she come
to the hospital
and wake me
with a kiss?

I wait for her

all night
and all the next day.

She doesn't come.

I see Vera scurrying

down the hallway
with dirty sheets
and a bucket.

I ask her about Jeanne.

Her face falls.

I'm so sorry.
I meant to tell you.

Everyone is worried.

Her father has died,
and her mother is very ill.

She looks like
she wants to hug me.

She lifts her feet
not knowing where
to place
the sheets.

She won't be back soon.
She's taking some time.

Vera turns and walks
down the hall.

Jeanne

We bury Maman

in the cemetery on the hill.

Two names
on the tombstone.

My mother's body
in the ground.

My father's body
lost,
in an unknown land.

I kneel down
on the grave,
place my hand
on the loose soil.

I wish I could
dig down
and lie with her
in the same bed
just like
when I was a child.

I waited so long
for Papa to return.

Now I know,
it is hopeless to wish
for things

that will never happen.

I arrive at the hospital

It's a cool night.

I pull my shawl tighter
around my shoulders.

I can't stop
shivering.

*What will Giorgos say
when he sees me?*

I don't know
if I can even say the words.

Both of my parents are dead.

For a brief second,
I imagine
that he will ask me
to marry him.

I turn the corner
and stop.

Gio's bed is empty.

I search
the other beds
frantically.

I look for
his books
his jacket
his watch.

Finally,
I ask the head nurse.

They shipped him out
two days ago.

Healthy enough
to go back to the front.

No note

No goodbye.

Did I imagine everything?

I have no one.

Who will love me
now?

Letter #20

November 9, 1918

A storm is coming.

The wind sounds like the rumbling wheels of a freight train.

From the window, I can see the giant oak.

It's been standing in this courtyard for three hundred years.

Swaying with each storm but not going anywhere.

Petit Oiseau

You must have had dreams

when you were my age.

Didn't you, Mama?

She stops cleaning the dishes.

Wipes her hands
on her apron
and sits down next to me.

Sometimes
the thickest dreams
become just
thin air.

Then
only the birds
can use them
to fly.

A second meeting is arranged

I can hear
my parents talking
and clinking glasses
in the kitchen.

I see my father
peer around the doorframe
to check on me.

To make sure I'm behaving.

Dimitris leans closer.

He places
his heavy hand
on my thigh.

A lion trapping
a mouse
under a paw.

My skin shivers.
My eyes turn green.

Please, don't.

I try to move
away from him.

I wish there were a rock
to scamper under
and hide.

His grasp tightens.

*You should feel grateful
that I want you.*

It is at this moment

that I decide.

I am not
a *Good. Greek. Girl.*

I am
a *Modern. American. Woman.*

There is nothing
my father can do
to make me marry
this heavy-handed
predator.

I will do as I please.

I stand from the sofa
and straighten my skirt.

Reach for my glass
and look Dimitris in the eyes.

I pour
an entire glass
of sour cherry liqueur
over his head.

Call me Athena

I live on Mount Olympus

and you
are only a mortal.

My father cuts a branch

from the weeping
willow tree.

I sit in the snow
to ease the pain.

Not a single tear shed.

It was worth it.

The next night

my father stumbles
though the door.

He weaves
through the hallway.

Calls me
and my mother
to his side.

Belt loose.
Shirt hanging.
Hair sticking up.

We can all smell
the firewater
on his breath.

His slurred words
ring through the house.

That man is an outrage!

No daughter of mine
will marry that beast.

      Giorgos, what happened?

My mother
talks to him
in calming tones.

Smooths his hair.

He insulted me!
He insulted our family!

He would be
LUCKY to have Mary.

Such a smart girl.
A loving girl.

LUCKY to have us.

He deserves to marry
a goat!

I don't wait
for him to change his mind.

I run
to embrace him.

Mama
comes closer.

Baba teeters
on his toes,
puts his arms around us,
and kisses the top
of my head.

You are my only daughter

It is my job to protect you.

I need to find a husband for you.

Don't I?

Don't I?

We let the question ring in the air,
a bell tolling.

A sunrise.
A prayer.

An announcement.
A new day.

Emboldened

I tell my mother

I want to own a business
someday.

She laughs in my face
and tells me

to change Pierre's
dirty diaper.

On your feet, soldier!

I look up and see an officer
standing over my bed.

I wipe the sleep
from my eyes.

You're shipping out today.

What are you talking about?
I can barely walk.

He looks at me
with steely reserve.

Orders.
Pack your bags.
Departure at 7:15.

I look at the clock
on the wall.

The hands read
seven o'clock.

Fifteen minutes.
Are you crazy?

Pack your bags, private!

Unless you want
to be court-martialed
instead.

I scramble to write Jeanne,
but there's no time.

I'll send a letter
from the road.

I feel the breath of the wolf

smell
the foul stench
from his jaws.

I hear him
snarling behind me.

I must return
to the front.

The hair
on the back of my neck
rises
in fear.

Jeanne

I sit naked on a chair

cover my breasts
with my hands.

A nun stands above me
with a knife
in her hand.

She begins to saw
the silver blade
through my long braid.

My aunt has given
all of my father's money
to the church
to ensure my care.

I have nothing.

It wasn't so long ago

I was playing
with dolls
on a balcony
overlooking the sea.

Now,
our house on the hill
is gone.

My parents
are gone.

I will live in the convent
where my aunt resides

and wear the
white veil
of a novice nun.

I return to my cell.

My body shivering
on a small cot,
covered
in a thin blanket.

I do not want this life.

I do not want this life.

I feel like a silent scream

I wake.
I pray.

I work.
I pray.

I eat.
I pray.

I sleep.
I pray.

And then
I do it all
again.

The aging priest motions

for me to sit
on the scarlet sofa
in his office.

I stare at the ornate
gold frame
holding a photo
of Pope Benedict XV.

His wire-framed glasses
almost hide
his sad eyes.

Jesus looms above me,
blood seeping from the wound
on his side.

The priest sits
behind his heavy black desk.

His robes
the color of heaven.

Are you ready to say your vows,
my child?

I look down,
my hands folded
in my lap.

    Yes, Monsignor.

Good.
We will set a date
for the spring.

That night, I dream

that I am naked.

Handcuffed and chained
in the town square.

Heretic!

The villagers
gather in a circle
around me.

Nonbeliever!

They jeer
and throw objects.

Witch!

A man pulls me
onto a platform.

He ties me to a wooden pole.

There is kindling beneath
my feet.

He lights a torch
and holds it close.

Save me from the fire,
I whisper.

The platform slowly
begins to burn.

There are quiet moments

that break through
the ice
of grieving.

Moments
when I feel
the Spirit moving
in the hallway

as my robes brush
against
the stone floors,

when I close my eyes
and hear all of the women
singing
in unison.

Moments
when I climb to the top
of the bell tower
and look at the sea.

Moments
when I wake
in the middle of the night
and feel that my parents
are very close.

Moments
when my only task
is to sit and read

and fill my mouth
with hot barley soup
and buttered bread.

Moments
when I walk in the graveyard
and the sun is setting
and I remember
the way my life
used to be.

When I miss Giorgos

my white veil

feels like a noose
around my neck.

The more
I struggle,

the tighter
it gets.

Letter #21

November 10, 1918

Dearest Petit Oiseau,

When I walk through the villages, I see all the damage that has been done.

Bombed churches and schools and homes.

When I think about the repair that will happen—when the war is over—it gives me hope.

I build towns in my mind.

Replace glass and repair fences.

Plant the window boxes with red flowers.

I imagine men and women working together to rebuild their towns and restore beauty with layers of plaster and paint.

Your loyal and loving,
Loup

Billy takes me to see

Diego Rivera's
commissioned murals
at the Detroit Institute of Arts.

The garden courtyard
opens up
with arches and columns.

We gasp and hold hands

as the light
floods in
from the ceiling
windows.

Shines
on the colorful images.

In each direction,
a progression.

The history
of science and technology.

We study
each of the four walls.

Spin in a circle.

East, north, west, south.

Each direction
describes
the history of our town
in images.

We turn to the east

where the sun rises,
a beginning.

An umbilical cord
runs from the earth
to the mother
to the child,
held in the bulb
of a plant.

The midnight swirl
of clouds.

The blood
of a new generation
works its way
into the soil.

Grows
like tuliped ears
of corn
bursting from its silk.

The mother holds
golden blue
apples
to her breast.

The mother braids
wheat flowers
into her amber hair.

There is growth
beneath
the surface.

The fruit is full.

Harvested
on the table.

Plenty for all.

We turn to the north

in the direction
of darkness.

The interior of things.

Mining of
coal and diamonds,
sand and limestone.

The motor assembled.

The blast furnace
glows orange
in the background.

Molten steel
poured into molds.

Men wearing gas masks
isolate substance
and dream.

A child in a manger
receives medicine.

Engineering.
Precision.

Invention.

We turn to the south

wall of light,
exterior of things.

The assembly
of the body.

Maintenance
of the body.

The goddess,
creator and destroyer of life,
maintains balance
and demands sacrifice.

Buildings
cobbled over
the extinctions
of past life.

Women organize.
Men calculate.

Humans watch
as the story unfolds.

Ford himself
stands over
the toil.

Push and pull
of the factory line.

We turn to the west

where the sun sets.

Endings
and judgment.

Passenger planes
and bombers.

Technology.
Destruction.

The hawk and the dove.

On either side
of history. [32, 33]

The men and women around us

whisper
under their breath,
shield
their children's eyes.

blasphemous
> *pornographic*

> > *foolishly vulgar*

a slander to Detroit workingmen

> > *coarse in conception*

> *un-American.* [34]

I see none of this.
I see my town.

Races working side by side.
Industry and history.
Medicine and religion.

Fertility goddesses,
giving birth to life.

Billy buys

a box of popcorn
from a vendor.

It's a sunny day.

We sit on a bench
and eat
the warm, crisp kernels
sprinkled with salt.

After we're done
his lips are shining
with butter.

He puts
his hand on the small of my back
and draws me closer
to him.

He kisses me.

And I feel it
everywhere.

After a moment, he pulls apart.

I saw an advertisement for a job
that I think
would be great for you.

He hands me
a square
cut from the newspaper.

I squeal
and grab for the scrap.

I press my lips
to his
and won't let him
come up for air.

I let Billy drive

me home.

He opens my door
and I sink
into the leather seats.

For months,
I've wondered how
it feels
to ride in this car.

Billy steers
with one arm around me.

Can I see you again soon?
he asks.

I look at him
with a determined look.

Eyes narrowed
and focused.

      Only if I can drive.

He laughs
in approval
and gives my shoulder
a squeeze.

I close my eyes
and feel the sound
of the engine
rumble
through my bones.

 Giorgos (Gio)

U.S. ARMY, NORTHWESTERN FRANCE
1918

The U.S. Army

has deemed
my body whole.

My mind fit.

I am not
the same soldier
who marched
these paths
so many
months ago.

A boy
eager to belong.

I am splintered
into a million
shards.

Mind filled
with violence
and pain.

My entire life
has been a story of loss.

Women push carts

filled with dresses,
pillows, and china.

Villagers dump
their belongings
in the streets.

All they cannot carry.

A man walks
with four horses
tied to ropes
trailing behind him.

There is human feces
in the road.

Everyone
is running away
from the German
border.

We are marching
toward it.

I close my eyes

and see Jeanne
on the beach,
light shining
through her auburn hair.

She's holding
a shell to her ear.

Her skirt
curves around her
in the wind.

She's searching for me.

Remembering me
in the trapped sound
of the waves.

I find a post office

It's abandoned.

Letters strewn
across the floor.

News
that will never arrive.

Words of love
that will never be read.

I stare at the letters in my hand.

Pray for everyone
who is lost.

Jeanne

I wake to the bells

in the tower,
ringing incessantly.

Are we being bombed?

I get dressed as quickly
as possible.

All of the other nuns
are gathered in the hallway,
looking drowsy and
confused.

Sister Agnes
comes bounding
up the stairs,
screaming
at the top
of her lungs,

We've won!

And just like that—
the war is over.

People are embracing

shouting
and laughing.

There's a band
marching in the streets.

Snare drums,
trumpets, and tubas
followed by a man
beating a big, round
bass drum.

I walk the town
alone
in my white veil.

I may be
the only one in the world
not celebrating.

There are so many soldiers

and they are all waiting

to get their
deployment papers
home.

Everyone is restless.

I see two men fighting
in front of the hospital.

A woman yells,
Stop, Jacob!
as one man hits
the other man
square in the jaw.

Blood spurts
across my white uniform
as I pass them.

I am shaking as I enter
the large, steel gates
of the hospital.

We need to find something
for these men to do.

The volunteer nurses
and I decide
we should hold
one last dance.

It is almost Christmas

We decide
to hold a snow dance.

A large tube
blows confetti
from the balcony.

White snowflakes fall
on the dancers
below.

All the other girls
look beautiful
in their long dresses
and ruby red lipstick.

I stick out
with my black robe
and white veil.

At intermission,
the nurses serve
hot roast beef sandwiches
pickles
sugar-coated beignets
nuts, chocolates
and cigars.

Sixty gallons
of hot chocolate
and not a drop left.

Everything tastes divine. [28]

When the music begins

the horns start blowing
and the strings start singing
and the snow starts falling.

I imagine
Gio holding me.

Kissing me
on the back
of the neck.

I close my eyes
and I feel his arms
around me.

We sway softly
in the middle
of the dance floor.

Until I realize,
it's not a dream.

I gasp
and turn around.

Gio's eyes
are shining with emotion.

He takes my hands
in his.

I squeal and kiss him

and then realize
my mistake.

I push him
away.

Where have you been?

> *They sent me to the front.*
> *I didn't want to leave you.*

You didn't even say goodbye.

> *I wrote you, but I couldn't send the*
> *letters.*

He places a stack of envelopes
in my hands.

> *I love you.*

I hug the letters
to my breast.

> *When they released me*
> *from my post,*
> *I traveled directly to the hospital.*

> *I couldn't wait to see you.*

> *They told me you were here.*

> *I love you, Jeanne.*

I can't love anyone.
I gave myself to God.

He touches
the veil
that covers my hair.

Why are you doing this?

His voice is not
unkind,
but I can tell he's angry.

I choose my words carefully.

I don't have a choice.

I take a deep breath in
as he says,

What if you did?

He reaches into his pocket
and pulls out a box.

I open it.

Inside, there is
a necklace.

A small golden bird.

I can't go home

I want to make a home with you.

Come with me to America.

The next day, my aunt

calls me
into her office.

She squeezes her eyes,
rubs her forehead
with her hand.

In one month,
you will say your vows,
and then you will be married
to God.

If this is not what you want,
you need to tell me.

Now.

Letter #22

November 11, 1918

One moment, I think I understand what the future holds.

The next moment, I realize that I don't.

Yours forever,
Petit Oiseau

My mother and I are doing laundry

when a neighbor
arrives at our door,
breathless.

There's been an accident!

My mother is shaking,
searching for coins
for a cab.

Our car is parked in front
of our apartment.

My brothers are nowhere
to be seen.

Silently, I take my mother's hand
and lead her to the car.

I open the door
and take my place
behind the wheel.

Mary!
You don't know how to drive!

She's standing on the sidewalk
refusing to get in.

I open her door
from the inside
lean over the seat
and say,

Get in the car, Mama,
or I'm going to the hospital
on my own.

When we arrive at the hospital

my father is mumbling
in Greek.

Get off me, you fools!
I have to get back to work!

But no one understands
this pitiful,
wounded man.

His words seem like nonsense.

Both of his hands
have been wrapped
in gauze mittens

and he looks like
a newborn
who is moving
its limbs
uncontrollably

trying to scratch
the skin

and scream
into the ears
of everyone
he loves.

My father has lost both of his thumbs

in a metal press
at the factory.

He won't speak
to anyone.

He lies splayed on the bed
like a wreck, scattered
on the side of the road.

He keeps repeating
the same phrase
over and over
in Greek.

I want to go home.
I want to go home.

An hour

turns into a day,
a day turns into a week,
a week turns
into two.

I bring
my father tea
that cools
untasted.

Toast
that goes
untouched.

He lies
with his back
to the door.

He will not move
from his bed.

Aunt Violetta sends a letter and a ticket

on a steamship.

New York City
to Athens.

My brother needs to return
to the olive groves
of his youth.

He has been gone
far too long.

Our eyes widen
as we read the words

My son and I
will return with Giorgos
when he is well.

My mother holds the letter

and reaches for me
with her other hand.

She looks slightly baffled
as she says,

I've never had a sister.

I want to say,

*I had a sister once
and it was the best
feeling in the entire world.*

I stop myself.
I don't want to spoil this.

I just hug her
as tightly as I can
around her waist.

The platform fills with steam

eardrums bulge

with the screech
of wheels grinding
to a halt
on the track.

My father appears lost.

My mother
pats his pocket,
reminds him
to board
the correct train.

The *Wolverine,*
from Detroit
to New York City.

I wonder how
he will make it
across the ocean
alone.

Right before we say goodbye

I pull
a stack of letters
from my coat
and hand them
to my mother.

Her eyes widen.

Where did you get these?

> *I found them
> in the cellar.*

Have you read them?

> *Every single one.*

She blushes.

Then rubs her palm
over the smooth
surface
of the envelopes.

> *Was this you?
> Are you "petit oiseau?"*

Yes.

> *I never realized
> you wrote letters during the war.*

We were so scared.

Alone.

We needed each other.

My father
puts his arm around her
and kisses her
on the cheek.

We still need each other.

Why don't you talk about the war, Baba?

Tears well up in his eyes.

It's over. Done.

His voice breaks.

The past is better in the past.

He squeezes
my mother's shoulder again.

I have what I need—
what I wanted all along.

You were a nurse, Mama?
Why didn't you continue?

Why didn't you tell me?

I became a mother
and that became . . .

You
became the most important part
of my life.

She hugs me.

I stand between them
and see
how much they value
our family.

How long they yearned
for peace.

How much
they love each other.

And me.

I watch my father board the train

He looks back,
waves,
and blows a kiss
to my mother.

A young man
saying goodbye
to his sweetheart.

Only this time,
she knows he will return.

I try to imagine
what it is like.

This land
my father loves.

The land
of my ancestors.

The land
I have never seen.

Giorgos (Gio)

SAINT-MALO, FRANCE
1918

I post a letter

to my sister and mother.

Heading to America.

The line at the ticket office

winds
out of the door.

Families yearning
for a new life.

I purchase two
transatlantic tickets
with all of my savings.

I hold them
in my shaking hands.

Jeanne

We gather in the courtyard

My aunt and Vera
stand beside me.

I close my eyes
and imagine
Maman and Papa
holding me.

Solid as an oak tree.

The monsignor
binds our hands
with a white silk scarf
and pronounces us

husband and wife.

Two days before

New Year's Day,
we travel by train
to Cherbourg.

The same harbor
where I said goodbye
to my beloved Papa
so long ago.

I turn
and say goodbye
to the country of my birth.

Gio hands the attendant
two second-class tickets
and we board
the largest ship
I have ever seen.

I try to look brave,
but my stomach lurches
with the waves.

We walk up
the lavish, grand staircase
of the *RMS Olympic*.

Porters take our bags
to our small room.

It has bunk beds,
a stiff sofa, and a tiny
porcelain sink.

We sit in a dining room
with molded ceilings.
White linen
and crystal glasses.

They serve
roast beef
with horseradish cream
mashed turnips
and cabbage.

After dinner,
we walk the promenade.

The wind is blowing.

I hold Gio's gaze.

*I want to work
when we get to America.
I want to be a nurse,
maybe even a doctor.*

*Tell me we won't let life
get in the way.*

Never, he says,
and pulls me closer.

I move into
the warmth
of my husband.

His dark eyes
full of expectation.

The convent feels
an ocean
away.

I have something for you

I say, and place
a stack of letters
in his hands.

I wrote to you too.

Mary

Letter #23

November 11, 1918

I had a dream of a seed, small and round.

What is this? I asked.

A voice said, "All that is made."

"How can it last?"

The voice answered, "It lasts and ever shall.

Everything has its beginning in love." [35]

Always yours,
Petit Oiseau

Without my father

once again,
our pantry is bare.

I tell my mother,
I will go
to the Ford factory
to find a job.

I expect her to laugh
and say,
They're not going to hire
a girl!

Instead,
she holds my shoulders
and kisses me
on both cheeks.

Is this what you want?
she asks.

      Very much, Mama.

If God wills it,
I am willing to let you try.

I put on
my best Sunday suit,
lace up
my high-heeled
boots.

I drive myself.

I arrive at the Ford factory

and take a moment
to breathe.

I smooth my skirt.

I reach down to
to tighten my laces,
and I see
something glinting
in the dirt.

I dig it
from its lodgings.

It's a round coin
on a chain.

I wipe the dust
on my leg.

There's a picture of a girl.

It's Jeanne d'Arc,
my mother's namesake.

Jeanne's hands
are clasped together
at her chest
with the words

Écoutez les voix
Listen to the voices

carved into the metal.

I remember the day
at the movies so long ago.

My sister
sitting beside me.

I hang the coin around my neck,
press it to my body.

It feels like Marguerite
placed this here
just for me.

I spin the radio dial.
Listen for the frequency.

I hear her.

I walk into the hiring office

at the Ford factory

and talk with the woman
behind the desk.

She's got horned-rimmed glasses
and a mug of steaming coffee
in her hand.

I ask her
if there are any
positions available.

I hand her my resume,
which only has
my foreign name,
my address,
and the high school
where I just graduated.

She looks at it
as if it were garbage.

Puts down
her coffee mug.

Shuffles though
some pages
without even looking
at them.

There is no work
available
for young girls
with no experience.

I take a deep breath in
and say,

*I saw in the paper
that Mr. Ford
was looking for an
elevator boy?*

A sharp burst of air
escapes her lips.

*He's been through
five people in the last
two months.*

*You see, he's very picky,
and that position
has never been given
to a woman or a girl.*

*It even has "boy"
in the job title!*

I ask to see her supervisor

He is a tall man
with a thin mustache
and oily hair
combed back
on his balding
scalp.

I tell him that my father
has been injured
at the factory,
and I have come
to replace him.

He looks at me
like I am a visitor
from planet Mars.

Then he points
his long, crooked finger
out the door.

I stomp

out of the office
into the lobby.

I see red.

My father was injured
on their factory floor.

How can these people
sleep at night?

How do they think
we are going to eat?

They don't give a damn
about their workers!

It's lunchtime

and there are hundreds
of people milling about.

I can't see over the heads
of the men wearing suits
and factory uniforms.

My body is jostled
back and forth in the crowd.

I end up getting pushed
into an elevator.

Eighth floor, please

says a man in a gray suit
from behind a newspaper.

We're the only people
on the elevator,
so I press the number eight
and close the door.

I look around.

The elevator is decorated
with mirrors,
red velvet, and gold.

I've never been in a room
this gilded.

It's shooting
through the sky
like a star
with wings.

The man folds his newspaper
and tucks it under his arm
and takes his hat
from his head.

It's then
that I realize.

I'm on an elevator
with Henry Ford.

When the elevator reaches the eighth floor

my hands start to shake.

The bell chimes,
and I slide open the gate.

I know I have to say something.

He steps off the elevator,
and just as
I'm closing the door,
I stop
and pull the door
open again.

Mr. Ford?

He looks up
with a surprised expression,
as though he's never
been addressed
by a woman before.

     Yes?

Mr. Ford,

I look at the man
who I admire
and fear.

The man who built
our town out of
metal and smoke.

I take a deep breath
and surprise myself
by saying,

How did you know?

   Know what?

*How did you know
you were going to change the world?*

Mr. Ford raises his eyebrows

and a small smile
blooms
on his lips.

What's your name, young lady?

> *Mary, sir.*

Do you work here?

> *Not yet, sir.*

He pauses,
and I can hear
the second hand tick
on the golden watch
dangling
from his pocket.

Well, I do need a new elevator boy.

I look him straight
in the eye.

> *How about an elevator girl?*

He looks
into the mirror
and straightens his tie.

He turns back to me.

*See you tomorrow at 9 a.m.,
Mary.*

I close the door

and press
the lighted circle
with my fingertip.

The golden metal box
slides down the side
of the building

like a burning ball
of light
sinking into the horizon

waiting only
for the opportunity
to rise
once again.

Giorgos (Gio)

KOMNINA, CENTRAL GREECE
1934

We heave the weight together

pushing
with all our strength.

The sea
rises up to our thighs.

Jump on!

My nephew,
Costas,
yells as he hefts
coiled ropes
into the hull
of the *kaiki.*

We jump into
the sturdy boat.

My boat.

Costas
smiles at my sister
as he stands on the deck.

His strong arm
on the tiller.

We fly across
the harbor.

A white Pegasus
with wings
for sails.

I stand in the olive groves

and inhale
the smell of the earth.

I can hear
the church bells
chiming
in the distance.

There is an ocean
between me
and my family.

I kneel down
and take a fistful
of dry soil
in my hand.

I will take it with me.

Across the world
back to my home.

Jeanne

My daughter

drives away
in a car
by herself.

I hear the boys
outside
playing ball.

The house feels
empty.

I feel the loss
of my children
more and more
each day.

The taller and wiser
they become.

I wonder,
after years
of giving myself
to my family,

What will I do now?

I enter the hospital

and walk
to the receptionist.

The woman looks up
and smiles.

Does she remember me?

From the night
I sat in this lobby?

When I held
and rocked
my feverish girl?

Does she remember?

The moment,
when the doctor
opened the blanket

looked at my daughter
and told me,

She's gone.

I try to keep my voice calm

my spine straight.

I look her in the eyes
and say,

I am a nurse.
I was trained during the war.

I would like to help.

Mary

Tomorrow

is the first day of my new job.

I lie in bed
and think about
Billy's proposal.

His kind blue eyes.

What would it be like
to have a name
like Smith or Jones?

Opera tickets.
Dinners and movies.
Honeymooning.

I think about growing older.

What kind of life
will I have?

A house of my own.
Children.

Working
and raising a family.

What will I do
with this freedom of mine?

Anything I want.

In my dream

air fills my lungs.

My chest
rises and falls.

I can hear
my city breathing.

Up and down.
Rise and fall.

In my dream

Marguerite
and I are flying
over the river
that cuts through town.

We travel
with the current
until we can see
the entire
country.

The rolling hills of wheat
swaying in the wind.

The mountains
pushing upward.

The rivers spilling
their waters
into the ocean.

The swell
of the stars close
above us.

In my dream

I can see my father
and his sister traveling
over the ocean
on the wings of the wind.

I can feel
the joyous breathing
of the people,
land, and sky.

In my dream

I know our family
in the heavens

and with our feet
on this glorious land

are finally together

traveling toward
the sun.

AUTHOR'S NOTE

Although this book is based on the family stories that I heard growing up, I changed the actual events quite a bit.

I never knew my great-grandparents (Giorgos and Jeanne), so the details of their journeys from Greece and France are based on a few historical documents, research, travels to Europe, and stories from my grandmother and her siblings.

I tried to transport myself to the early twentieth century and visualize what these characters would have experienced during that time. Then I tried to create a narrative with twists and turns and engaging imagery.

My greatest hope is that I represented my family well and that they would have been pleased with this book. At times, the story became so strong and insistent that it felt like my ancestors were whispering in my ear, telling me what to write. And I *listened to the voices*.

Mainly, I wrote this book for my grandmother Mary, who became a successful businesswoman in the 1950s, when women usually never entered the boardroom. She rocked the pantsuit at a time when women were expected to wear aprons and pearls.

She never let her misfortune hold her back and always summoned the courage to do what she needed to do, even when she was afraid. I see this as one of life's most valuable lessons.

My grandmother could tell a fantastic story—she could hold an entire room with her humor, her intellect, and her infectious, high-pitched laugh.

She would tell us about her childhood in Detroit, Greektown, the Ford factory, the poverty her family faced, and how she had to fight for her independence.

The same story was never the same twice, but we loved listening to the rich details and the passion that was embedded in every word.

She died at the age of 92. After years of struggling with Alzheimer's, she forgot almost everything about her life. But her stories live on—in our memories and in this book.

My Great-Grandmother Jeanne (Jeanette) Skandalaris, my Great-Grandfather George Skandalaris, my Great-Uncle Gus, my Grandmother Mary, and my Great-Uncle John.

Apparently, this picture was considered a failure by Jeanette, because Mary couldn't stop wiggling her foot—the photograph was blurred.

Mary Skandalaris (age 18), around the time she became Henry Ford's elevator girl.

Mary Smith (age 21), shortly after she married Bill Smith.

Mary (age 92) hugging my daughter, Phoebe, just a few months before she passed.

This is a manifest from the *RMS Olympic* (sister ship to the *Titanic*!). My great-grandparents are numbers six and seven on the list. In my novel, the characters Giorgos and Jeanne travel to the U.S. in 1918, not 1920, but I wanted to keep this ship because I love the history. The actual *RMS Olympic* was in service from 1911 to 1935. From 1915 to 1918, it was used to transport Canadian and U.S. troops to Europe.

Note that my first name, Colby, also appears on the manifest twice in the porter's handwriting. This was one of the many reasons I felt called to write this story.

NOTES

1. The woman speaking at the church is quoting Matthew 19:24.

2. The lines on the signs in this poem are inspired by a photograph of two children living in a "Hooverville." https://www.thirteen. org/wnet/historyofus/tools/browser12.html

3. Lines quoted from "The Three Little Pigs" by Joseph Jacobs's *English Fairy Tales*, published in 1890.

4. A Hooverville was a shantytown built during the Great Depression by the homeless in the United States. Hoovervilles were named after Herbert Hoover, who was the president of the United States during the onset of the Depression and who was widely blamed for "the downfall of economic stability and lack of government help." u-s-history.com

5. "Keep That Wedding Day Complexion" was a line from a Palmolive ad printed in *Ladies' Home Journal*. https://repository. duke.edu/dc/adaccess/BH1209

6. "Promiscuous Bathing" was the title of an article written by Felicia Holt in *Ladies' Home Journal* in August 1890.

7. The *fête de Noël* music scene was inspired by "The Goadec Sisters." https://www.youtube.com/watch?v=lSWwHQXt0d8

8. The language that Mrs. Patterson uses to describe the Ford factory and Detroit was adapted from a promotional film released by Ford in the 1930s, "The Harvest of the Years." The term "City of Transportation" and the phrases "forge and lathe / work and tend / spin and weave / form and transform" are from this film.

9. Father Yiannis quotes 1 John 3:16.

10. The Fox Theatre in Detroit was one of America's first movie palaces. This prominent Detroit landmark was recently renovated and is now open to the public for events and concerts. The movie *Mary, Marguerite, and Jeanne* watch at The Fox was inspired by *The Passion of Joan of Arc*, a classic silent movie from 1928 directed by Carl Theodor Dreyer.

11. The American Coney Island is one of the oldest businesses in the downtown area of Detroit. It was founded in 1917 by Constantine "Gust" Keros, who immigrated to Detroit from Greece in 1903. The restaurant has remained at the same location for 97 years.

12. The phrase "donkey of the sea" and the quote "It is better to get where you are going rather than rush and not get there at all" came from this article, https://www.kavas.com/blog/traditional-greek-vessels.html, written by Richard Shrubb (https://richardshrubb.com/).

13. The line "watch the tide come in as swiftly as a galloping horse" is borrowed from Victor Hugo, who was also inspired by Mont Saint-Michel.

14. World War I nursing scenes were inspired by: *Nurses at the Front*, https://www.nfb.ca/film/front-lines-nurses-at-the-front/. Nothing was directly quoted from this film, but this short documentary helped me gain an emotional understanding of wartime hospitals during this time.

15. Some of the nursing poems were inspired by Nurse Edith Appleton, from Deal in Kent, England, who kept a diary while working at General Hospital No. 1 detailing the Battle of the Somme. The poem "We don't hear exact numbers" and the line "stinking and tense with gangrene," as well as the last two stanzas about the blind boy, are all adapted from a passage in her journal. More of her letters can be read in the book *A Nurse at The Front: The First World War Diaries of Sister Edith Appleton* (Simon & Schuster).

16. The Hunger March poems were inspired by the article "Diego Rivera's 'Battle of Detroit'" by Tom Mackaman and Jerry White, which includes the quote: "We put four of your kind in their graves with this and we'll put a lot more if we have to." https://www.wsws.org/en/articles/2013/10/03/indu-o03.html

17. The vehicle numbers and the story about the diamond cufflinks came from the *Detroit News* article "How the Great Depression Changed Detroit" published on March 3, 1999.

18. The unemployment rate in Detroit in March 2020 (when I wrote this book) was 4.86 percent, and the unemployment rate in April 2020 was 22.7 percent.

19. Southwest Detroit Auto Heritage Guide provided the quote: "No Ford or Dearborn officials were prosecuted for deaths caused by the gunfire." https://www.motorcities.org/southwest-detroit-auto-heritage-guide/ford-hunger-march

20. The line "too much jitter in my jitterbug" was inspired by this article about ballrooms in Detroit during the Depression: http://blogs.detroitnews.com/history/2002/01/20/when-detroit-danced-to-the-big-bands-8/. I adapted my line from the line "too much 'jig' in my jitterbugging."

21. The Eleanor Roosevelt quote about flying came from the article "First lady rides the night skies with Amelia Earhart as pilot" published on the front page of the *Baltimore Sun* on April 21, 1933.

22. The Ellis Island scenes were inspired by a ferry boat ride to Ellis Island and the Statue of Liberty National Monument, where I was able to find record of my family's immigration into the United States.

23. Belle Isle Park is a beloved 982-acre island park located in Detroit. It's a great point of pride and is still in very active use. Notable highlights include: Belle Isle Aquarium, Anna Scripps Whitcomb Conservatory, Dossin Great Lakes Museum, Belle Isle Nature

Center, and the James Scott Memorial Fountain. https://www.
belleisleconservancy.org/

24. *Celui que mon coeur aime tant* is a traditional sailor's song, a *chansons des marins* from Brittany, France.

25. Restrictive covenants were written into housing deeds to discriminate against racial and ethnic minorities. Blacks who were brave enough to purchase homes in white neighborhoods often suffered violence. One of the most famous examples of this brutality is Dr. Ossian Sweet, a graduate of Howard University and a physician. In the summer of 1925, he purchased a home at 2905 Garland Street, an all-white middle-class neighborhood. An angry mob swarmed his house, threw rocks, and broke windows. Shots were fired from inside the house, killing one man and seriously injuring another. Sweet, his wife, and their associates were all arrested and charged with murder. His house is now a National Park site. https://www.nps.gov/places/dr-ossian-sweet-house.htm

26. The Detroit Eight Mile Wall, or "Detroit's Wailing Wall," was built in 1941 to physically separate white and Black homeowners to ensure the neighborhoods were segregated. The wall is half a mile long and ends just south of 8 Mile Road, which is a stark symbol demarcating the segregation of 78.6 percent Black Detroit and predominantly white Macomb and Oakland suburbs. In 2006, a portion of the Wailing Wall was covered in a mural by residents and community activists, highlighting images of Rosa Parks, Harriet Tubman, colorful houses, and children blowing bubbles. The mural serves as a recognition of the past but also as a symbol of hope. https://www.census.gov/quickfacts/fact/table/detroitcitymichigan,MI/PST045219

27. The list of baby superstitions was adapted from an article originally published on greekweddingtraditions.com. I wish I could thank the author who gave me the inspiration, but the website is no longer working. So, I shout "thank you" into the ether and hope it will be heard.

28. The details from the moon and snow dances, and the line "slick as a ribbon," were borrowed from a letter written January 18, 1919, by a World War I nurse named Orena English Shanks Bourne. Bourne served with the American Expeditionary Forces in France. Excerpts from her letters were printed in a Louisville, Kentucky, *Courier-Journal* article entitled "Hot chocolate, dancing eased wait after WWI" written by Nancy Stearns Theiss on January 12, 2016. The letters were donated to the Oldham County Historical Society, where Theiss serves as the executive director.

29. The poems about Ford's politics and working wage were inspired by the article "Motor City: The Story of Detroit" by Thomas J. Sugrue, published September 16, 2014, by The Gilder Lehrman Institute of American History.

30. Henry Ford once remarked: "I am more a manufacturer of men than of automobiles." The description of Giorgos's first day at the factory was inspired by Henry Ford's "Melting Pot" ritual at his Ford English School for employees who were immigrants. Ford built an actual melting pot made of wood, canvas, and papier-mâché. He hoped it would "impress upon these men that they are, or should be, Americans, and that former racial, national, and linguistic differences are to be forgotten." tenement.org/blog/adapting-to-america

31. "There's a Ford in your future" was an advertising slogan that was used by Ford Motor Company in the 1940s.

32. The poems about the Detroit Industry murals were adapted from the descriptions of the individual panels by Linda Bank Downs in her book *Diego Rivera: The Detroit Industry Murals*, published in 1999.

33. You can see the Diego Rivera murals at the Detroit Institute of Arts and also on its website: https://www.dia.org/art/collection/object/detroit-industry-north-wall-58538

34. On March 19, 1933, a *Detroit News* editorial called Diego Rivera's murals "coarse in conception . . . foolishly vulgar . . . a slander to Detroit workingmen . . . un-American." The writer wanted the murals to be "whitewashed." npr.org/2009/04/22/103337403/detroit-industry-the-murals-of-diego-rivera

35. Letter #23 was inspired by the Catholic mystic Julian of Norwich. She had visions when she was dying: "And in this he showed me a little thing, the quantity of a hazelnut, lying in the palm of my hand, it seemed, and it was as round as any ball. I looked thereupon with the eye of my understanding, and I thought, 'What may this be?' And it was answered generally thus: 'It is all that is made.' I wondered how it could last, for I thought it might suddenly fall to nothing for little cause. And I was answered in my understanding: 'It lasts and ever shall, for God loves it; and so everything has its beginning by the love of God.' In this little thing I saw three properties; the first is that God made it; the second is that God loves it; and the third is that God keeps it."
— Chapter V, *Revelations of Divine Love (Westminster manuscript)*

ACKNOWLEDGMENTS

Several years ago, a fellow writer and friend, Abigail Rayner, asked me, "Have you ever thought of writing a novel in verse?" This question changed the course of my life. Without her encouragement, close reading, and advice, this book would not exist.

I would also like to thank my past, present, and future students at the Arts Council of Princeton: Annie, Martha, Hope, Jen, Charlotte, Stéphanie, Barbara, Carol, Mary, Jeanette, Joanne, Jessica, Regina, Beejay, Fran, Kathryn, Nuria, Anne, Donnagail, Ken, and Claire. Thank you for your encouragement, camaraderie, reading, editing, and advice. You keep me writing and inspired.

Thank you to my loving and creative tribe: Abby and Béla, Erin and Cory, Maria and Eric, Paula and Adam, Wandee and Jon, Maria and Urs, Kate N., Emily F., and Clare S. Though we live in different corners of the world, your influence on my life and work has been immeasurable, and your support and love has always been boundless.

Thank you to my Hopewell/Princeton sister-friends: Ellie, Emily, Nicole, Jess, Bridgid, Andrea, Ali, Debbie, Kendra, and Alanna. And the whole Snyder/Finn-Bario crew. You all keep my feet on the ground. Thank you for helping me to raise my babies while I build a bridge between the world of the living and the world of ghosts. It really does take a village, and you are mine.

Thank you to all who gave me sound counsel: Henry Reath, Margery Cuyler, Yoshi Okamura, Patricia Hruby Powell, Suba Sulaiman, Roseanne Wells, Andrea Cascardi, Jen Henderson at Studio JPH, and Bobbie Fishman at The Bear and the Books. Thank you to my wonderful sensitivity readers/editors: Elina Gouliou (Greece), Stéphanie Larotte-Namouni (France), Sarah Brangwynne (Orthodox), Ceylan Akturk (Detroit/First Generation), Renee Halstron (Black/Diversity).

Thank you to all the mentors at Rutgers University Council on Children's Literature and the New Jersey chapter of the Society of Children's Book Writers and Illustrators, especially my former agent, Larissa Helena, who was the first person in the industry to believe in this book. Thank you for your astute editorial advice and unwavering support.

Thank you to my professors: Joan Stone, David Mason, Dana Gioia, Lucie Brock-Broido, and Jorie Graham, who taught me how to be a poet; and Steve Seidel and the Arts in Education department at Harvard Graduate School of Education, who taught me how to be a teaching artist and an advocate for social justice.

Thank you to my agent extraordinaire, Allison Hellegers, who worked tirelessly to edit this manuscript and find a home for the book during a global pandemic. Even while you were spinning a million breakable plates in the air, you kept me laughing and calm the entire time. I am grateful to you, and to Stimola Literary Studio, for giving me a home.

Thank you to my editor, Patty Rice, and the folks at Andrews McMeel Publishing. Your commitment to editing and designing beautiful books is astounding. I will be forever grateful to you for manifesting my dreams and making this real. Thank you for believing there was an audience for this book. And thank you, Ruta Sepetys. Your kind words of praise and genuine letter of support were life changing for me. Thank you for lifting me up.

Thank you to my mother, Jan, my father, Jim, and my sister, Darcy. Your voices of love and encouragement are ever-present. You have shaped me into being, and I am forever grateful that you are mine. Thank you to the Schoene, Bayly, Regele, Langohr, Baker, Broome, Marquis, and Rodriguez families for accepting me and loving me as your own.

Thank you, Phoebe and Saylor, my bluebird and sailboat. You give my days meaning. You inspire me to create and allow me to love more than I ever thought possible. Thank you for listening and questioning and for being the most funny, sensitive, shining children that I could ever imagine.

Thank you to my magnificent and brilliant husband, Blair Schoene, who has read every poem I have ever written. Thank you for taking me on adventures. Thank you for challenging me and encouraging me. Thank you for helping me to be brave. You are my heart.

And finally, thank you to the readers, the creators, the innovators, and the dreamers. You inspire me every day. And thank you to the brave souls, like Jeanne and Gio, who risk everything and come to the United States to search for a better life. We are stronger because of your courage, hard work, and dedication. You are the soul of our nation.

Colby Cedar Smith grew up in the Midwest, and she still dreams of the cold northern woods and the smell of lake water. She holds degrees from Colorado College and Harvard University. In 2020, Colby received a New Jersey Individual Artist Fellowship in Poetry. Her poems have been published in *Bellevue Literary Review, Harper Palate, Mid-American Review, Pleiades, Potomac Review, Saranac Review,* and *The Iowa Review.* Colby lives with her husband and two children in New Jersey, and teaches creative writing at the Arts Council of Princeton. You can read more of her work at www.colbycedarsmith.com. Follow her on Twitter: @ColbyCedar, and Instagram: @Colby_Cedar_Smith.

Enjoy *Call Me Athena* as an audiobook, wherever audiobooks are sold.